THE

LIZARD WOMAN

THE

LIZARD WOMAN

FRANK WATERS

SWALLOW PRESS

OHIO UNIVERSITY PRESS

ATHENS

First Swallow Press/Ohio University Press
paperback edition printed 1995
02 01 00 99 98 97 96   5 4 3 2

This book is printed on acid free recycled paper.

Library of Congress Cataloging-in-Publication Data

Waters, Frank, 1902–
    [Fever pitch]
    The lizard woman / Frank Waters. — 1st Swallow Press/Ohio
 University Press paperback ed.
        p.   cm.
    Rev. ed. of: Fever pitch. 1930.
    ISBN 0-8040-0987-2 (pbk. : acid-free paper)
    I. Title.
 [PS3545.A82F4   1995]   94-42346
 813′.52—dc20   CIP

Contents

Preface

THE LIZARD WOMAN, under the title of *Fever Pitch,* was published in 1930 by Horace Liveright, New York. It was an immediate flop and soon went out of print. A cheap paperback edition selling for 25 cents, issued in 1955, did nothing to redeem it. Not until now have I permitted another reprint. The book was my immature first novel, betraying faults I was hesitant to see exposed. This is false pride, of course; one is reluctant to admit early ignorance and ineptitude, as if a writer miraculously falls heir to competence in his craft without any preparation at all.

The novel was begun in 1926, when I was twenty-four years old and working as a telephone engineer in Imperial Valley, on the California-Baja California border. During my stay there I made a horseback trip down into the little-known desert interior of Lower California. After having lived all of my early years in the high Rockies of Colorado, I was unprepared for the vast sweep of sunstruck desert with its flat wastes, clumps of cacti, and barren parched-rock ranges. Its emotional impact was so profound, I was impelled to give voice to it with pencil and paper.

Every night after work I settled down to write in the two-room shack I was renting in El Centro. Its plank walls were waist high, to the top of which canvas flaps could be let down from the roof in daytime to shut out the blazing sun, and pulled up at night for air. During the summer when the thermometer climbed to 110 degrees or more, the place was hot as an oven. In the winter, with no heat save the kitchen stove, it was cold as a refrigerator. The shower room was a wooden hut in back. Upon opening the door I turned on the electric light, then waited for the cockroaches, large and hard-backed as turtles, to scurry away. The water when I opened the fawcet was cold and muddy red as the Colorado itself. As the saying was, one took a bath and brushed off with a whisk broom.

On summer evenings I walked through town. Swarms of moths fluttered around the street lamps. Droves of ground crickets from the desert covered the pavements. So one walked the cottony desert streets of night. It was like walking through a hospital ward. On the withered lawns row upon row of figures lay sleeping on their blankets. Then home to write. . . .

I began with a description of a remote desert valley enclosed by barren rocky mountains, around whose circular rim lay the semblance of a gigantic lizard with a woman's face meeting the end of her scaly tail.

This fantastic description was the middle of the novel, beginning Part Three. What then confronted me was the problem of inventing a beginning and an end to whatever story could enclose it. The enveloping narrative I contrived was an adventure story somewhat like the common pulp-paper Westerns, but told through a narrator as were many of Conrad's great novels of the sea. This adaptation seemed natural, for the desert always reminded me of the sea.

The writing itself was a chore. In college I had majored in engineering, without taking a course in English or literature. As a result most of us engineering students were unable to write an application for a job without copying a form letter. My own narrative I arbitrarily divided into long and short paragraphs merely to avoid the monotony of unbroken pages. The dialogue was awkward, the punctuation capricious. The story of only two characters in an empty desert, to whom nothing dramatic happened, gave me trouble. I found myself using the desert and the Lizard Woman herself as the main character. This, after all, was my reason for writing. So I did not hesitate to indulge in long descriptions.

All these faults, not obvious to me then, were glaringly clear in the finished handwritten manuscript. I laboriously typed it the following year when I was recalled to Los Angeles, and sent it to the most prestigious publisher of the time. Horace Liveright accepted it, and suggested editorial changes. Objecting to my title *The Lizard Woman,* which he considered ghastly, he changed it to the really ghastly *Fever Pitch,* and finally published it.

Yet for all its faults, *The Lizard Woman* had one redeeming virtue. As Thomas J. Lyon has pointed out in his critical analysis of my writing, it anticipated in a strange way a major theme of my later books.

Not until years later did I discover that I had unconsciously projected in my description of that imaginary desert valley of the Lizard Woman one of the oldest symbols known to mankind—the *uroboros,* the circle formed by a serpent biting its own tail. Its hieroglyph in ancient Egypt designated the universe embracing all heaven and earth. The modern psychologists C. G. Jung and Erich Neumann interpreted the *uroboros* as the symbol of primordial unity, enclosing the infinitude of all space and time; the Greek *pleroma,* the fullness of divine Creation. The serpent itself, linking the beginning and the end, symbolized timeless time.

How clear now was the meaning of that remote desert valley enclosed by barren rocky walls, around whose circular rim lay the semblance of a gigantic lizard with a woman's face. It was the universal image of the uroboric serpent projected from my own unconscious. It was all there, complete, although I had not known of it nor understood its meaning.

The symbol stuck in my mind. Long afterward, during my short tenure at Colorado State University, I gave a public lecture on "Mysticism and Witchcraft" which was recorded and published in an attractive booklet. For the cover I selected the symbol of the *uroboros.*

Still later, while I was in Mexico doing research into Mesoamerican mythology and religion for my book *Mexico Mystique,* I learned that the ancient Aztecs believed that the earth rested on the back of a *cipactli,* a saurian monster of some sort: crocodile, serpent, or lizard. The earth was a flat disc surrounded by a great ring of divine water that merged with the heavens above. To this circular earth surrounded in turn by a circular world-pool of water, the Aztecs gave the name *Cem-Anahuatl,* the "complete circle." From this was derived the name of Anahuac for the Valley of Mexico, the Aztec homeland. So here again in Nahuatl cosmography we see the uroboric components of the wholeness and fullness of all space and time.

Is the primordial perfection of Creation also symbolized by the Christian myth of the Garden of Eden, from which Adam and Eve were banished because they ate the apple of the tree of knowledge? In eating the apple, man gained the faculty of rational thinking which is the basis for our present Western civilization. But he lost the immediate, intuitive apperception of the universal completeness, unity, and harmony of which he had been a part. Yet this primordial wholeness is still retained in what Jung calls our "collective unconscious," its symbol of the *uroboros* emerging into consciousness through dreams, visions, and imaginary fantasies.

Excessively rationalistic and materialistic, we have stifled the intuitive truth of how closely we are linked to all nature, the earth, waters and the stars above. The *uroboros,* to whomever it occurs as it did to me, offers the promise of universal unity that still lies within us waiting to be regained.

Enough of these post-mortem comments on my first book, published more than fifty years ago!

We are grateful to Ohio University Press for republishing this book, and hope that its future will be as enduring as this old tale of the Lizard Woman has been in the past.

Frank Waters

The White House

✳ I ✳

SAY WHAT YOU WILL, for those who spend their days upon the desert the solitude has a voice which forever cries in their ears. . . . So for this tale make of it what you will, for it is the tale of Lee Marston, a man; Arvilla, a woman; and the Lizard Woman, who was neither.

It was there, upon that white-washed, up-stairs porch of La Casa Blanca, that he came to us, as did Eric Dane's words themselves; infinitely sad, indefinitely aloof, like the dim, un-real figure of a tale alone. He was standing in the doorway of that little Border cabaret; squinting as though dazed by the sudden brightness of the flickering jet above him. And as he paused for a moment on the dusty landing we seemed to see in his face all the foreboding silence of the land itself, all the unruffled depth of that vast pelagic plain which surged about us. His hair, as he removed his hat, we could see to be dried-out, yellowish-white in the evening breeze. The usual old trousers and the clean white shirt he wore were ordinary. It was his face which again drew and held our attention by its simple, unique singularity of expression. He seemed young. His face was young. And then we began to doubt its telling, for it at once spoke of a man whom time with both youth and age had passed unnoticed. It was all serenity, but not that of years: rather did it reflect the calmness of one who has been drawn into the imperturbable serenity of earth and stars. Only the hard brightness of the man's eyes clashed as he ambled across the room. Slightly built, he came toward us like the tossing of a rudderless ship on a swelling sea, turned slowly, and fitted silently into the lee of a far table on the opposite edge of the porch.

"There," Dane settled back into the shadows, "Lee Marston, the man I was telling you about."

It was the hour of sunset. Silently we four sat through the glorious moment which like the momentary spring of the desert cannot be measured in time. There on the porch, across the table, was Dane, dark as any shadow. There was Ellsworth, eyes and ears for him alone. There McHenry, hands as impatient as himself. And there, out over the balcony railing, there beyond the adobe walls of that Mexican border town, far even as the sunset, lay the desert itself of which we were speaking.

"Yes," Ellsworth had just answered, "yes, I believe that is true. Somehow I always feel like that for the split-instant that I turn from the mountains to strike down into the desert. Until then I am aware enough of the approaching desolation, and my eyes, my sense-eyes if you know what I mean, are attuned to the outdoors. But the minute the desert closes about me—it does, as you say—all those things pass from my mind. Then I am conscious only of a presence, a very real presence, of what seems to be an embodiment or the inexorable spirit of the land itself. You've felt it, McHenry, always complaining that the heat followed us like a swarm of flies. And the night we awoke when you asked me if I couldn't brush the star off your nose. But to admit the possibility of its actual effect, Dane—well, I don't know."

Eric Dane, grim featured and slow of speech, shook his head, "And why not? Take Marston for an example. For only one reason, perhaps, Marston's tale cannot be laid to the desert, the land itself. It carries in due justification the thread of his own sensitive nature. There also was Arvilla, and the Lizard Woman whom he himself can hardly explain. Yet with all this, there is something, the very existent, tangible reality of the earth from which we emerged; something, with the faint, dying echo of an immortal strain which is blown to us all."

The sun had cast its last flare into that upstairs porch which overhangs the hot, dust-filled street below. Upon the white-washed adobe walls still hung the quivering heat-haze of the afternoon, and brought the Chinese bar-boy at frequent intervals to fill our glasses.

"I never heard such a man," McHenry drummed good-naturedly upon the table at us, "as Dane here. Observant, analytical as a judge, and argumentative as the Devil himself. What chance would he have, this Lee Marston, what with your reasons against, and all of it like pages from a book?"

Eric Dane slowly pushed across the small bottle.

"You can't fool me, McHenry. There's more than only facts. With only the facts a man can judge nothing: for in the grip of power which existed before even man, a power strong as the hand of Creation, flexible as a breeze, a dream without form, facts are as the sands of a storm, blown any-whither by the fancies of their holders—"

"Oh come, Dane."

Still later to us watching Lee Marston that night at dusk, he seemed strangely aloof, curiously detached, removed forever from our immediate understanding. He held our gaze with the same paradoxical, compelling attraction that a dim charcoal sketch so often has. A very chiaroscuro sort of man he was, arm on balcony, staring down into the dusty street below. And even as we listened to Dane, the circumambient desert, the encroaching sense of its vast stretches of loneliness, rolled in upon the street. Like his manner, Dane's voice was easy, purposeful, restful with the ease of repression. Even McHenry relaxed gradually, came to ease. And, eyes fixed upon that quiet figure before us, we listened to his tale.

✳ II ✳

To Lee Marston watching the darkness settling slowly and intermingling its gaps with the dust, that evening must have been as now; the evening he met Arvilla. Down there the street stubbed its same crooked length directly into Yee Wo's Loncheria. All your mean little cantinas were blossoming like night-flowers in the dark. He saw the rosy painted front of La Gloria; the purple adobe walls of the Tivoli; the faded, yellow Chinese lanterns hung from the doorway of the Cantina Shanghai. Farther down flickered the colored three balls of Las Tres Luces. Up to him floated the clatter of wild piano keys from the blazing white and noisy El Palacio. From across the street flaunted the tainted streamers of tequila, new Azteca beer, and mescal juice, all in that feverish, alcoholic stink of a little crawling street on a hot night.

Along that twisted alley-way below him Marston said had streamed the nightly mass of faces bobbing up and down like brown corks in a slow stream of dust. Brown Mexican laborers *en famille;* gaunt turbaned Hindu melon pickers; shiny negroes from the new cotton fields; men from off the desert; white workers like himself of all types. But of them all, he confessed to waiting for the dark, untroubled features of the men from off the desert as he watched them ride slowly past.

The desert, the land. That was what held him. Like the sea, its illimitable expanse had gripped his imagination. There was no shutting out the insistence of its brooding, brown waves of sage and sand breaking toward the hazy horizon. By the hours, by the nights, he has sat and talked to me: of his first childhood fancies of that receding, unapproachable horizon; of his first railroad survey; of finally, the Lizard Woman, Arvilla, and those things whose beginning lay within the night he sat alone upon the balcony porch.

Always he seemed like a man newly awakened from a troubled sleep, as though without thought of the thing that tantalized his still sleeping memory. It had no form, nor could he give it birth of shape. Always it was there just beyond his grasp to trouble his thoughts like a quirk of conscience.

He was capable enough even then. The Company engineers left no doubt of that. Perhaps he was more restless than the others. Relieved a week or so from work he was ready again for the field. He moved from camp to camp as the survey progressed. Only sometimes he might have been seen standing for just a moment looking away into that hazy, wavering line of sky and sand that troubled him so with a quizzical, half-humorous expression on his face, like that of a man who suddenly remembers the time of an appointment long overdue. Yes, he was like that; like a man possessed by a dream for which he could find no form.

He was right.

In those barren solitudes he found something; and as its telling returns to me and I see him now, I know that his tale is not mine. And sometimes when the night draws about me close as the soft folds of a heated blanket and it is I who am alone, I feel that the tale is, after all, not alone his. For it partakes of those things beyond the reach of his understanding and ours. And yet, though he is again alone, he is not lonely; living in a maze of unreality which to me seems not always of his own making. His very solitude, it seems at times, plays for his ears its own music which not even I can understand.

But as I say, it was the night he met Arvilla. He said the porch door opened. The light from that inside cafe room struck across the table like a felled tree, little branches and leaves of light fluttering in the shadows of the porch. A small Chinese boy paused before the table, an almond-eyed lad with the smooth yellow face of an old lacquer piece.

"Hello, Hen'y Li," said Marston. "I guess you can bring me out a little bottle of that cheap red wine until I cool off enough to eat."

The boy vanished into the lighted room wherein sounded the dull whir of fans, the sputter of light jets, and the noisy clatter of the filling cabaret. Marston turned to watch him. Faintly there came from across the floor the clink of coins as the evening gambling began. Dark men with green eye-shades passed up and down behind the écarté dealers; the ring of Mexicans deepened about the panguingui table. Echoes of "Pocar Robado," Draw Poker; "Pocar Garañona," Stud Poker, resounded through the room. A dicing machine in a far corner broke into the sound with a cacophonous clatter.

All these Mexican cabaret affairs along the Border have their girls, swarthy creatures of the night who live from beer check to bar scrapings. So also had La Casa Blanca. In answer to the noisy summons of a piccolo, guitar, violin, and flute, they gathered on the floor. A scraggly row of brown Mexican percentage girls, they filed out to the center and, spasmodically, began to kick and dance.

One of them caught Lee Marston's idle gaze. It was Arvilla. He watched her closely. She had a dancer's legs, the torso of a toreador, and the face of a brown Madonna. The moving lines of her figure, as she swayed in unison with the screechy music, stood out ineradicably from the row of dancers. She could have been a series of pen and ink sketches drawn from wall to wall so swift and clear she stood apart from the rest whose sodden faces were empty as their own beer schooners.

Not too soon the players stopped. The music wailed sadly to silence and the clatter of dice began again. The girls scattered, straggling towards the long bar or picking out escorts for the next dance.

Marston's glance followed Arvilla as she eased up to a drunk, pock-marked Mexican and began to wheedle for a drink. Swaying unsteadily from foot to foot, he threw her off and clasped his bulging shirt pocket. The girl laughed and began to stroke his arm; then she made a quick dart into his pocket. Her fingers caught in the cloth and tore it open. A few escaping pieces of silver fell to the floor and rang loudly. The Mexican, firm on foot at last, turned and swung a heavy fist. The blow tumbled her to the floor. And then Lee Marston saw what had seemed to place her apart from the leering, jeering faces crowded about the floor. There was no cowardice about her, none of the abject decay of the cantina-woman. One of the others would have arisen and slouched quietly away, but not Arvilla. Like an animal she was crouching, right hand to bare brown thigh. Her face was dark with grim determination; she seemed wrapped in the calm, inflexible stoicism of her race. Her hand crept forth with a knife, bright with an unsuspected glitter.

It was over instantly. Someone in the crowd, a fat panguingui dealer behind her, caught her arm and knocked the blade from her hand. As the crowd surged forward, Marston saw the frightened face of the Mexican vanishing unsteadily through the doorway. He caught a glimpse of something else between the bare legs of the dancers. Arvilla had replaced the long knife and her brown hand was scraping over the floor in search of the abandoned silver.

Lee Marston pushed back his damp hair and turned his cheek to the first faint stirring of the evening breeze which swept up to the balcony from the street, still warm, carrying the dim, evil winks of invitation from the cantinas which one by one leapt into sight.

Some time later the door squeaked open behind him. At his side he heard a step toward the table.

"Set it down, Hen'y," he said, 'and then I guess I'll have some dinner."

Instead, a soft arm was laid over his shoulders. He looked up. The percentage girl from inside was standing beside him. He shook off her arm.

"Here! None of that," he said.

She flopped down in the chair opposite him and leaned across the table. "Cómo no, Señor?" she asked. "How not? You weesh I was the bottle, per'aps, yes?" Her voice was soft, flat as stale beer.

"No," stated Marston. "I'm not sitting up here waiting for a bottle of tequila to get drunk on, if that's what you mean?"

The girl laid a brown hand on his arm. "Ah, yo lo creo. I can well believe it. The Señor weeshes a girl, eh? You weel dance with Arvilla, then? A very nice dance for one dreenk?"

7

"No, I don't want to dance with you. Here, beat it! You can't make any money off me. Go in and try somebody else with a clean shirt. Maybe they've got some money for you."

He slid a coin across the table top. Deftly it slipped into her hand, and Marston could see the warm length of her leg as she dropped it into her stocking. A shadow fell across the table and dropped over her stockinged leg. At a motion from Arvilla, Hen'y returned with a second glass and began to crack the ice. Marston looked up in surprise as she motioned him away and began to pour the wine. To it she added something from her long, sinewy fingers.

"Too much ice," she said, "will spoil the Señor's wine. Mucho frio, it is bad. See, two cloves is like much ice and will make him wish me to stay. No es verdad? Perhaps the Señor is lonely, not wishing to dance with Arvilla?"

Something in the smooth decisiveness of her face stopped the command which rose to his lips. He took up his glass. The infernal nerve of these cabaret girls! But as he sipped at the wine and noticed the cooling effect of the cloves, he leaned back and was still. Rather slowly he began to answer the girl's determined questions. "I'm not going to get drunk. I don't want a percentage girl. And I'm not lonely. As a matter of fact I was just watching all this while Henry brings me some dinner."

Of course he was lonely. He waved his arm vaguely out over the balcony railing. Darkness had settled slowly, removing in its folds the dusty upstairs porch from the splotchy row of colored lights below. The peak toward the west and south was a monstrous shadow of the night, formless, imponderable. Above it hung two pale stars. Marston spoke again, almost to himself.

"Those stars," he paused, "seem more real than those bright buttons on your dress."

Arvilla leaned forward across the table. The indolent slouch of her figure was gone. She stared into his face. "Ah, el desierto! You theenk of the desert? You are going into the desert? Per'aps in those rock mountains which go down into Mexico? 'Los Llanos de Los Perdidos,' 'The Plains of the Lost' they are called.

Come with me! I too go to the desert again. There I will show you gold. Gold! Great flakes of it! We have waited for you. You weel come, Señor?''

Lee Marston looked at her slowly. Arvilla as the dancing girl, the percentage girl was gone. Her face, brown with a pristine smoothness, had set in a calm mask. Determination, strength, a ruthless will, were written in every contour. Her lean brown hands gripped his wrists.

"Ah, but you will not let me go alone? Come with me! Por la Madre de Dios, may all the curses of the Lizard Woman be upon you eef you do not go!"

Lee Marston sat up. The ring of her words echoed in his ears. "The Lizard Woman," The Plains of the Lost," called to his fancy strange images as though they were vaguely familiar. He reached down to unlock her fingers. In the soft stream of light across the table he saw the dull flash of an ornament clasped about her brown wrist. It was a heavy gold bracelet of peculiar form, and he saw it was beaten in the likeness of a lizard whose flaked tail was wrapped round her wrist and whose head was the face of a Mexican dancing girl.

In itself the thing was insignificant, almost without interest. But to Lee Marston that bauble was always a talisman. Ever afterwards he had only to look at it to arouse a sort of mesmeric wonder. For it was portentous; a key to the locked door of his memory; a personal sign to him from his own created infinity. It was as a crystal ball in which, clairvoyantly, he seemed to see the flicker of his stars, the guiding lights of those symbols of life by which his course had long been set. . . .

✳ III ✳

ARVILLA CANNOT BE EXPLAINED. With her lazy days, riotous and greedy nights,. and the inevitable black-paper cigarette between her lips, she was a type known too well along the Mexican border. Yet there was something about her that couldn't be classed. A mestiza, she sometimes was wholly Indian in a sort of barbaric abandon of indifference. Drink affected her like that. She was never nervously, screamingly drunk. All day she just lay as though stupefied in some adobe doorway. By night you would see her head down on a cantina table with those big, dark eyes of hers shining bigger and darker than ever through her cigarette smoke, still open and unwavering.

At other times she seemed to give herself to the sinuous workings of some dark stream of Mexican desire that cried for possession in her mind. She was like a spoiled child crying for a bauble. Once her greedy eyes fastened upon a bright colored zarape, a braided belt, or the most trivial object, all her indolence was gone. She could not rest until it was hers. She squirmed about like a beautiful snake for its possession, smiling, and rubbing up close to you with an outstretched hand. All her body gave, but not her eyes. They jumped and glittered and told you "look out" in tones twice bigger than life.

Yet there was something in her more noble than her nature; something of the truth, surely, was within her. Perhaps not. But she was a woman and Marston never forgave her that. Even as he watched her face through the thick smoke of her execrable black-paper cigarette he was aware of its Madonna-like serenity of expression. A dark face, compelling of outline. She was pleading swiftly now with a rush of Spanish phrases and English slang.

"Oígame Vd. Listen to me. Why do you not listen to my words? Do I not tell you—

"Say," he spoke slowly, "I didn't get all that. Talk so I can understand you." He took up her arm. It was warm; the soft down was slightly damp. "This bracelet thing. Is this the Lizard Woman you were talking about?"

"No-no-no, Señor Le' Marston," her voice rose quickly with his name. "Not this. Only un amuleto, a charm you say, of the gold from the land of the Lizard Woman . . . For he said when he gave it to me, that of hers all things return. And it is this which will take me back across Los Llanos de Los Perdidos and over the Mountains of Fire. Ah, Señor, you mus' go with me quickly, for he is waiting and soon the sun will be of fire."

Marston bent his head and fumbled for his glass. He knew that the girl was playing for a heavy percentage chip on the dinner of rice and beans con carne she had ordered. They all did. Yet in her words he caught a harsh sincerity. All else she heard with the indolent manner of one whose business it is to assent to all things. But at the mention of the desert all the mannerisms of the cantina entertainer vanished with her immediate response of interest. Her face seemed to grow more brooding, more silent. He felt in her presence the indefinite, undeniable dry strength of vast stretches of desolation. The will of her, her ruthless determination, interjected itself into his feelings. As if the mere mention of that remorseless world stripped her of all trivialities.

"No," he replied. "When I said I was going over the desert, I meant I was going back over the desert. That's enough, all right. I came in over it to work on this new railroad they're putting through. I didn't say I was going out prospecting. I'm just going back to the Division Camp and get another job before I lose all the money I have left of my last one. Savvy? So you'd better beat it back inside and start dancing again."

Even as he spoke he knew his brusqueness was futile; an unconscious desire to combat his own curiosity. The dishes had been cleared away; and Arvilla leaned toward him, resting her arms on the smooth wood of the round table. She nodded her head toward the cafe room with a gesture of disdain.

"Chihuahua! So you would have me dance, Lee Marston? Never, Señor, for now soon I will have enough money to leave. And with the gold of the land of the Lizard Woman, then will I never dance again. I shall have gold here and here"—the brown hand jumped over her dress from bauble to ornament—"and Arvilla the dancing girl will be no more. Escuche! Listen! Un ingeniero—a surveyor or what you say?—the Señor, who can melt rocks and say, 'This is gold. This is silver. Perhaps this is cobre of the rocks!' Don de Dios! A gift from God, Señor, who can do these things! It is what we wish. Listen to my tale.

"'Arvilla,' he said, 'return to me before the desert burns with the heat of the summer. With you bring one man. Tell no one else. Just one man who can melt the rocks and say for sure this is gold or this is silver or this copper, el cobre de las rocas. For you, for me, and for this man will then be all the gold of the land of the Lizard Woman.'

"See, Le' Marston? Gold, gold, great flakes of it on the Mountains. And for us he is waiting. Quickly I go. You will come? Madre de Dios! Tell me 'no' and I shall . . ."

"But who? I can't get you. Who is it who said all this?"

"Horne. Jaime Horne. El Hombre Conejo, which is to say the rabbit man. I call him that because like a rabbit the head above his eyes, which are big, is very flat. And his chin like this"—she chucked her teeth together with the back of her hand—"goes clip-clip-clip, like a cow who chews nothing, or a rabbit which has no grass. Listen! With him I went across the desert.

"Soon we were in the land of the Lizard Woman, and about us were many queer crawling creatures who came to drink in the little stream in the rocks which tastes like beer with much salt. Of this I can remember but little, for it was very hot. Hot, Le' Marston, as if the sun was a coal of fire laid here on this very table. But to me, Señor, Jim Horne brought little rocks in his hands, and he brought great rocks in his arms. And in each rock, little rocks and big rocks, were small pieces of gold. Little pieces of gold for Arvilla to put on her dress, to put on her shawl as a Señorita of the land, little pieces of gold to put in big bags for you, Le' Marston, which will make you un gran hombre of your country!"

Her voice lowered slightly and went on. "About us were little animals, little birds of the bare rock hills and little caves in the rocks by the stream. 'Here will I stay, Arvilla,' he said to me, 'and gather great heaps of rocks from the hillsides. Return before the summer has come upon us with the man who can say this is gold. With me will stay the packs and with you will go the horse. With you shall also go this charm which will bring you back, for of the Lizard Woman all things return, for is it not a land of God who gave it to her in its making?'

"Back across the desert I came and here I have been many months, dancing for the money to buy many things. It is hard to dance, Señor. 'See,' they say, 'all bones and skin like a dead horse, and brown as an old rock! Give us a girl to dance with,' and my cheeks are white from many dark rooms. Look, Señor, it is not my legs which the sun made brown and hard."

Lee Marston shook off her hand and turned his eyes out over the balcony railing. The row of lights from the bars, cabarets and colored cantina-fronts glittered sadly down the street. The music of El Palacio borne by the evening breeze came in disheartened spurts of sound and died in a noisy clash. The yellow faded paper lanterns hung limp and dejected from the doorway of the Cantina Shanghai. The purple walls of the Tivoli were vaguely reminiscent of diluted, washed-out wine. Only the two stars above the gaunt peak toward the west and south were aglow with life. Aloof, coldly antagonistic, they looked. He shrugged slightly, an unconscious movement of which he was perhaps unaware.

Arvilla's eyes, he noticed suddenly, were large, so warm and brown. Her lips were full, warm too, doubtless. He shook his shoulders again and pushed back his chair.

"Here!" He tossed upon the table top two silver dollars. "Probably these were what you were after." He laughed shortly, looking down at the girl who was methodically slipping the coins into her stocking. "I guess I'll go to bed now that the breeze is up. Thanks to you I'll probably be dreaming about lizards with girls' heads all night."

He passed into the café room inside, head down, ambling without interest past the row of écarté dealers, the ring about the panguingui table, heedless of the resounding cries of "Pocar Garañona," "Change in!" which sounded in his ears. From the doorway, under the dim light, he looked back. The motion, if you can understand, was a tribute which he should not have paid. That he was to do later. On the outside, white-washed porch of La Casa Blanca at the small table on which stood an empty wine bottle, Arvilla was still seated, musing, alone.

✳ IV ✳

FROM THE COLORADO to the Gulf, Marston in his work had followed a well-beaten path. That the path was in reality only a matter of red dots on the maps of the company surveys made no difference. He knew the next one, after a day or so of traveling over flat stretches of desert, through hills of brown parched rock, or between immense thickets of chaparral, manzanitas, and scrub oak, would be sure to appear. A company supply camp or a pueblo of a few adobe huts. They were like beads strung on a long string suspended from the greasy mountains to the west over miles of desolation limited only by his own imagination. He felt that to drop on either side was to be plunged into the immensity of the land which stretched interminably beyond his eyes. Like a mighty palm whose jagged fingers were of baked ridges of rock, it seemed to hold an unsounded silence. The Salton Sink of legend cuddled to the north like a tiny drop in its hollow, and through its fingers of sand trickled the red and muddy Colorado.

To Marston it held something else. Never was it explained though the legends grew. The nights bred dreams and brought spectres. From somewhere, unnoticed, a man and his burro would suddenly appear. Gaunt, hollow-faced fellows who camped in the glow of their own fire, rods off, or else sat silent, watching with eyes that glittered like the metal they never found. Others spoke but said little and Marston never asked. Only in the mornings he watched them off toward the smoke-blue mountains with that expression of his that tried to build a dream.

In all his work from camp to camp, no tale until that night on the upstairs porch of La Casa Blanca had taken root like the tale of Arvilla's. It blossomed quickly and its flowers enticed his thoughts. Great gulps of blue mist and clouds of yellow dust. Mornings like moonstones and evenings like the heart of a desert rose. A sun like a copper disk and a moon like a silver crescent. The strange legend of a forgotten land within the heart of the desert. "Los Llanos de Los Perdidos!" As the days passed, the phrase returned with new significance. He put off his return to work from day to day.

Each evening as he sat at his accustomed table on the porch of La Casa Blanca, the last rays of the sun edged closer to his lap. Each evening Arvilla's remorseless pleadings grew stronger in his mind. It was a tale he completed as he lay awake each night long after the feet had ceased their shuffle past his door. The wild tale of a man abandoned in a lone, dead valley like a very pit of desolation, in a land abandoned by God and swayed by the power of a Lizard Woman!

James Horne grew real. To Lee Marston the mere fact of his alleged existence was sufficient. He was as a man of the imagination, true to every picture, a fantastic figure which grew with every word from Arvilla. A vast idealism enveloped him like a mist through which he loomed more clearly with every thought. Far across that glittering expanse he waited. Waiting for Arvilla to bring help and someone to tell him that what he had found was gold. Riches beyond his wildest dreams. Great flakes and nuggets of it, and a share to the man who proved it possible. A Midas of a man with the heart of the world for a realm. And the bracelet was tangible. It opened all doors, an omen of protection, the sign of faith. What a faith!

I wonder if Marston ever believed it all. Perhaps he never gave it a thought; surely not the gold. It was the other, this fancy of a man waiting for deliverance like a man not of this earth awaiting the touch of something tangible, earthy, to reveal him to this world. A man inside a dream, perfectly conceived, el hombre conejo, James Horne the rabbit man!

15

"You do not like me, Le' Marston?" Arvilla asked him one night. "You theenk I do not speak truth? Look, soon I will go!"

She pulled down her stocking and laid a soft leather band on the table. It was warm to the touch. She shook it gently and caught the coins which fell out.

"See, Señor, who does not believe my words?" Her brown fingers arranged the coins in many small piles. "With this shall I buy leather pouches, with these I shall buy water bags, with this many dried vegetables. Hammers to pound the gold, many clothes for the Señor Horne, camisas of wool, scarfs for the face when the sand flies, medias, zapatos."

Each night she would stack before him the day's coins and proudly, almost passionately, declaim their use. Each night her brown, Madonna-like face leaned closer to his across the small table.

"Ah, Le' Marston," her voice seemed to roll the 'Le' Marston,' into a sticky pill ready for swallowing, "you will go with me across the desert before summer comes? Alone you will go with me across the Mountains of Fire?"

Her voice, Spanish and yucca-sweet, caressed his senses. It lulled to rest all doubts. Reality vanished. Before her his logic dissembled almost before he thought of questions. He asked her for a sample of the gold; he asked why Horne hadn't returned with her; he asked meaningless questions all with that slow, disinterested, listless voice of his that never waited for an answer. But whatever she might have said would have made no difference.

Of the two, Arvilla was the stronger; and she was a woman. In everything she bore down his will by that one grasping tenacity that knew no defeat. Only when he turned away his face with that disinterested, dreaming expression was she powerless. Intuitively, perhaps, she remained impersonal and it was this which gained her point. Unconscious of appeal, her dark face pleaded across the table as she wrapped the leather coin pad above her bare brown knee. Only once, just for a moment, her body leaned against his, warm, soft, with almost a clinging texture in its appeal. Neither of them noticed it; surely not Arvilla. She was

16

promising him riches, he who had a dream richer than the gold of a summer sunset and as far away!

An hour later he saw her vanish through the door with the arm of a swarthy Mexican worker about her waist.

That night Lee Marston decided to go. . . .

Having once made up his mind, he began preparations for the trip with all the joyous abandon of a school boy on a vacation. For several days he let it be known that he was going on toward the coast. He had about two hundred dollars left from the savings of his last job. With it he bought two horses for himself and Arvilla. A perfectly matched pair of roans, slim-legged, well groomed, and with high cantled saddles to match. With the remaining money he bought two fine-grained saddle bags which he filled with fresh fruit. He was all enthusiasm. At night he walked down the dusty, starlit street remembering how warm Arvilla's lips had always seemed, her dusky tan, the soft clasp of her long fingers. "Once again I am soft for men to dance with," he seemed to hear her voice in the breeze and saw the dark eyes facing him. The lonely prospector Horne seemed far away, almost forgotten.

The two roans were penned in a small corral at the end of the street. Head and shoulders they stood above the other nondescript, scraggly ponies that had crowded them into a corner. Smiling, Marston said nothing as he opened the gate for Arvilla. He was going to surprise her. With sharp eyes Arvilla was appraising the jostling scared ponies when Marston nudged her and pointed to the horses.

"There they are, Arvilla. They're the ones."

Carefully she walked around the two horses, slowly, as if she would see past the glossy texture of their smooth skins.

"No buenos, Le' Marston," she announced curtly and turned back to a dirty small piebald.

Marston took her arm and swung her round sharply. "Here, Arvilla. What do you want with those dirty scrubs? These are the horses I've bought. The best looking animals in town!"

Arvilla's face hardened as she voiced her disapproval of the horses. "Carajo! For why you buy these scarecrow things to feed the buzzards, Señor?" She ran her hands up their long legs. "Their legs they break like a blade of dry grass. Mire Vd!" she gripped the nostrils of a fine head. "Too high they hold their heads. The sand, it will fill their noses like a breath of wind. I buy these leetle horses here; Arvilla who knows these things. You give me the money, eh?"

Lee Marston shook his head. Wholly foolish perhaps, excessively romantic, he could see Arvilla clothed virgin-like in the lace of a white mantilla mounted only upon one of the two great roans ready for his hand to lead away. Unargumentative of tone he told her he had already paid the money for the horses.

"Madre de Dios! You are a fool! What you theenk we do now? Where do we find lakes of water for these no-good horses?" She pointed at the beasts in the corner. "What do you put in those beeg bellies on the desert! You fill them with sand, eh?" She turned her head and shouted at the Mexican squatting against a post, "Oiga Vd! Venga aquí!"

The man rose and ambled toward them. Arvilla swore loudly, pointing at Marston and the horses and demanding the return of the money. Marston shuffled behind her and winked an eye at the Mexican. The man stood still. When Arvilla stopped talking, he insolently shrugged his shoulders. "It is as the Señor wishes," he said and slouched back to his post.

Arvilla whirled upon Marston. "Christ! Goddam to you, Señor! You are as a child who knows nothing. You will learn it is Arvilla only who knows, who has been upon the desert. Lo siento mucho. I am so sorry for you. Caramba!"

With what might have been the sign of the cross, she turned without further glance at the horses and walked away. Marston laughed lightly in a shamed-faced manner and followed her out the gate. In that laugh was the spirit of his starting: just turned nervous, yet light-hearted, unconcerned with other than that vision of himself and Arvilla on the two fast-stepping roans, alone, riding across the miles which stretched with a beckoning brightness to the limit of his colored imagination.

Arvilla, more like a mother on a business shopping trip, cautiously doled out thirty silver pesos and many "Nombres de Dios!" in exchange for a long-eared, shaggy burro which Marston said was small enough to carry. His instant dislike of that burro was almost symbolic; he never got over it.

Spring was slipping fast and the heat each night came in more intense surges from off the desert, and brought the Chinese boy at frequent intervals to fill their glasses. And it was Marston who now did all the talking as they went over their preparations. Arvilla only sat and stared, almost morosely, out over the balcony railing. The more elated Marston became, the more quiet she grew, more forcefully alert. It was as if at the mere thought of going her mind was slowly hardening to the trip, gathering her strength of will, husbanding her reserve forces. Each coin from the soft leather strap above her knee was laid on the table and its exact use determined, weighed in the light of possible necessity.

On the last morning she loaded four small kegs of water from the bar of La Mantilla, a quantity of dried fruit, and thin packs of clothes which she used for the pack blanketing. Not an ounce of weight which could not be used. In the very center of the pack, wrapped in a silk scarf and wool camisa, she placed the small black case of Marston's chemicals for assaying. She handled it carefully, reverently almost, as if it contained the holy water for the shriving of a man's lost soul; as though it alone were the means of withdrawing from an abyss of eternity and vague conception, a something to be treasured above all things.

The silent preparations, the utmost concern with which she made every move, disconcerted Marston. He would have forgotten the case himself. For the first time since he heard her tale, he recognized in her actions a grim forcefulness of character, the same ruthless determination of will, a certainty of an end. And it seemed suddenly strange that, after all, they were going for a purpose.

✳ V ✳

THE NIGHT, as they rode out of town, was soft as a mist and charged with a portentous blackness. The sky was like low-hung black velvet on which were worked small and protruding, silver-hard daisies. Marston and Arvilla, high on the two roans, rode side by side. The loaded burro behind them was led by a rope hooked to the cantle of Arvilla's saddle. Slowly they proceeded down the short street, unheralded by so much as the cry of a stray dog or a gesture of interest from a group huddled in the shadows of the last cantina.

They followed the railroad bed out of town until the faint twinkling of the lights behind them seemed smothered in the blackness, and the music of the cantinas was lost in the sweep of the breeze over their heads. Then they turned and entered upon a vastness Lee Marston felt to be illimitable in extent.

Even the two horses seemed to sense the unrestrained eagerness of freedom with which the air seemed charged, for they proceeded with long swinging strides and with noses which reached out straight before them. Only the top-heavy burro, like a burdened dwarf, and Arvilla jerked along like two shapeless automatons. The night was sweet and the breeze was cooling to their cheeks. The swing of the horse was always restfully forward, like a ship floating out on a heavy tide. Marston believed that never before had he experienced such exquisite fullness of perception. A suppressed promise seemed to drift over him expelling any vague uneasiness of the future. There was nothing he desired.

The slight pull of the rein in his hands filled him with a keen sense of mastery. As if only by the strength of his own hand was he resisting the urge of the night which drew them unsteadily forward. The ripple of the thigh muscles of the roan beneath him, the faint swell and fall of the sides of the horse, regular as the beat of a powerful engine, kept time with the swing of his own body in the saddle. Free from the guide rope of the burro which Arvilla was leading, he rode easily, always with that elated sense of freedom he could not restrain.

Arvilla, humped in the dark mass of a long black rebozo, rode head down, steadily forward. After a time she stopped. Looking to the guide rope of the burro and the girth of her own saddle, she began to fumble in the shawl for one of her long, black-paper cigarettes. Marston swung to the ground and flicked toward her a lighted match, an almost courtly gesture. The glowing light enveloped her face in a yellow haze. Her eyes, deep and black, stared calmly into his. He drew out a flask.

"Wine," he said, "kind of a stirrup-cup, you know, that I asked Hen'y to get for us before we left. Maybe we'd better drink it now. For you, Arvilla; I'm going to be good to you, Arvilla."

Arvilla, between puffs, drank deeply. "Gracias," she said simply. Lee Marston closed his own lips about the curved glass opening. When he looked up Arvilla was again bent over her saddle horn. Over her shoulders was flung the long rebozo which covered her head and hung to the stirrups. Silently he stood and looked up. A monstrous black figure of the night loomed before him. She was that unreal. A great hooded figure looking down at him from a height he would never reach. Shrouded in the voluminous folds of the shawl she had no form, no outline save that of beast and man, shapeless, without substance. Nothing but her eyes which for one instant caught the flash of the scudding moon. They penetrated him. Even after she turned, he could feel that glance imbedded within the sudden, hollow recess of his heart. It was searching, searching for an answer he felt he could never give. Arvilla as a dancing girl, a percentage girl of La Casa Blanca, was suddenly gone. Nothing but that remorseless, shrouded figure moving off without sound. She now belonged to the night.

He swung, somewhat stiffly, into his own saddle and settled himself to the slow swing of the horse. In time his head, like that of the burro, drooped lower and lower, bobbing with the stride of the roan like the bow of a ship in a smooth sea.

Through the night the two horses strode forward. Behind them, with the sporadic jerks of a somnambulist, the burro chugged steadily. The moon rose higher. It was pale. The stars had lost their glitter. It was as if the land, now lifeless, was bathed in the phosphorescence of a world without. The sky assumed a faint color, changed slowly from the portentous blackness to the indescribable pallor of washed-out lilac. The surface of the land, the flat top of the mesa, lay limp as the pictured surface of a dead moon. Clumps of desert growth stood out in curious detachment, widened into vast stretches of sand bleached in the faint color to resemble splotches of fresh fallen snow. The world was in a resounding harmony of silence, the spirit of a pervading desolation. It was there when the mountains to a ragged crest rose to life. Suns had crumbled the rocks, pale moons saw them rolled again to sand. Seas came and went, ever leaving the silence which now lay unmocked by any appeal of life.

A tiny sound broke into discord the harmony of the night. It was the sharp ring of a horse's hoof against a small rock. Arvilla raised her head, jerked at her bridle rein and again slumped forward over the saddle horn. A cactus wren flapped sleepily into safety some yards away. The plaintive cry of a night bird echoed from afar. Toward the mountains to their side the gray splotch of a coyote slid past. In the pale light which seemed to come from the sky and not the moon, clumps of desert mice ran swiftly over the sands. Soon all again was silence. The mountains across the mesa frowned with black shaggy brows and relapsed once more to slumber.

Once during the night a peculiar thought awakened Lee Marston. As if Arvilla were his wife. Not a sharp wave of desire, he understood. It was simply as if he had already drained her of all new raptures and were basking in the dying glow of a passionless heat which was to hold him secure for all time. He put out a hand to her at once. But she was riding quietly beside him, humped in the dark mass of the long shawl. He drew back his hand to the saddle horn.

Toward dawn the breeze died. The night like a locked room became suddenly close, stale as the taste of last night's tequila. It awakened Lee Marston. He looked about him. It seemed that he was riding in a fantastic mist in which only the sleepy realization of where he was seemed real. It forbade the memory of lights, of music, of sound. The unearthly pallor frightened him as he awoke. It was as if he were looking down from the immensity of the heavens upon a land beyond his comprehension. The growth about him sank from his sight; splotches of smoke trees merged into puffs of clouds even as he looked; the sage shrank to the shadows. He felt, curiously enough, that all things of the night hid his coming, a stranger to their midst.

Far ahead a mass of the wrinkled mountains jutted toward him like reefs of an open sea. Gulfs of the peculiar mist filled their open crevices, the opening cañons. Recurrently he saw tall pillars bunched on top. He finally made out that they were a clump of palms. As they grew to his sight, the unreality about him diminished. He fixed his gaze upon them, drawing closer with each stride of his horse like the anchor line on which a drifting sailor pulls to shore.

Arvilla was riding two lengths before him. She appeared to be sitting quite easily, almost erect. Behind him, the burro was slowly plodding after the horses. The lead-line, he noticed, was coiled neatly and fastened on top of the pack. He watched Arvilla. She, too, seemed to be riding toward the slender clump of the palm trees which stood out clearly, a landmark from afar. For an instant Marston felt a quick flash of resentment toward her. It was she who without a word, without deviation in course, had ridden steadily forward in the lead, holding the direction. Arvilla it was who once they were away had loosed the guide rope of the burro, knowing that it would trail slowly after them. It was she who had set their pace. He dug his heels into his horse to catch up with his companion.

The roan, almost sluggishly, started forward in a jerky trot; and by slow degrees he reached the shadowy mass of Arvilla, ever moving forward toward the palms which like a landmark in a shadowy sea stood out half-revealed behind the first faint veil of dawn.

✳ VI ✳

DAYLIGHT CAME IN A DIM, greenish-gold bath of liquid fire which drenched the moving figures of the beasts and the long, waving arms of the ocotillo and mesquite clumps around them with a weird ghostly pallor. In the dim green glow Marston's face appeared colorless, drawn out of shape, like that of a man dazed by an unreality too livid to be suppressed. He was never to experience that again. Its dark hours were as the essence of a dream in which only his senses played a part. It was as though through the long, calm beauty of that night he had seen ebbing on its vast tide all the musty fragrance of the crooked little street below La Casa Blanca, the sharp edge of his own enthusiasm, even the alluring beckonings of his dreams. And it was never to return.

Arvilla, for her part, rode easily as Marston had noticed some time before. Like two fighters held in leash they had been: Marston alert, joyous for encounter; Arvilla silent, preoccupied, reluctantly slow as if dreading the issue. Brooding and alone she had hidden behind a surly silence. Now, once launched and with a night behind them, she emerged from the mood which had possessed her.

"Es de día!" she called. "It is daylight. Buenos días, Señor."

Marston grunted a short reply. It had a coated-tongue sort of sound. Arvilla looked sideways at him in surprise. Tousled hair stuck from under his hat. He was slouched all ways in his saddle, and little beads of perspiration already stood out on his face in the sunlight.

"Bebamos! Let us drink," she told him, "for yet is the Cañon of the Palms many hours' ride. See, Le' Marston," she pointed between the limp ears of her horse, 'how in the daytime the sun is like many miles of the night. Were we not wise to ride in the night-time when the desert is asleep?"

They rested and ate in silence.

With the day came the heat; and they continued, feeling the flanks of the animals grow wet, and smelling the rancid odor of hair, leather, and dust. In the first yellow haze of day the brown, parched hills slipped away on either side of them toward the horizon. Before dawn the Cañon of the Palms had stood directly in their path. The arroyo walls, even the wrinkles of their sides, had stood out clearly. But now, after the metallic rain of sunrise, the valley walls were separated from where they stood by the shimmering folds of a vast silken sea above whose heat waves the shaggy tops of the palms rose slowly.

Soon after noon they approached the arroyo. Within a curve of the cañon they came upon a small ranchito. A desolate spot, for all the living green of an untended corn patch and some dusty fig trees, with its two huddling adobes.

One of the horses, sensing water, neighed shrilly. From a ramada the ragged patrón emerged and stood lighting the inevitable black-paper cigarro.

"Buenas tardes, Señor." called Arvilla.

The man approached slowly, without surprise, and took off his hat.

"José Barajas, servidor de ustedes," he announced himself in an old phrase. Marston dismounted and with Arvilla removed the saddles. As he gave a quick jerk at one of the buckles, the saddle bag flew suddenly open. A litter of fruit fell to the ground at their feet. Arvilla looked down at the tumbling array in surprise. There were a half-dozen overripe cantaloupes, peaches, pears, and other pieces of fresh fruit which had been shipped in as a rare and expensive bar display to La Casa Blanca. What they had cost, Marston and Hen'y only knew. Swinging loose against his leg and bumping with each step of the horse, the fruit had been bruised and crushed to a soggy mass.

Arvilla, noticing the angry dismay which flooded the face of Marston, remained silent. She turned to the group of children who had come from the adobes and now stood watching them, all absorbed.

"Para ustedes, muchachos," she indicated the fallen fruit. The children quickly gathered up the mass.

The evening passed quickly before a small mesquite fire between the two adobes. Around each open doorway squatted the rest of the family. The two daughters seemed to Marston as old as the ragged, aged Señora herself who sat wrapped in a dirty cotton rebozo which almost covered her face. Only the eyes of the children, small, moving, reptilian, expressed interest. The meal of roasted ears of corn and huge dry tortillas took little time.

Lee Marston lay back and was silent. He might have not been there, so strange it was, so far back into the recesses of his memory was the last night before their departure. Even the children drew from him to watch Arvilla as she sat talking with the patrón. Her words came rapidly and were absorbed by the listening circle before their echo reached his ears. The man spoke little. Once he pointed into the night.

"Quień sabe? Who knows? Diez—veinte—veinticinco—más o menos. Maybe more, maybe no."

It was noncommittal. Only the quick accompanying gestures expressed disbelief. Forgotten, Marston watched them talk. Later Arvilla turned and looked at him. Quite steadily. The smoke from her cigarette rose between her fingers and curled upwards past her face.

When she looked again, he was asleep.

✳ VII ✳

As THOUGH HE WERE awakened from a dream of the place, Marston again found himself out upon the desert. Memory of the ranchito was already only one sharp, clear-cut picture as an episode long past. Perhaps the clearest vision was that of Arvilla's face wreathed in the smoke of the cigarette in her fingers, like a face within a cowl. There seemed no immediate past, only the immensity of the land which fell away before them. At each step a puff of dust rose gently, sifted to a fine powder in the sunlight, and enveloped them in a blinding, scratching tissue of the land over which they passed without a backward glance.

To one side the low broken hills, which seemed like the outcropping reefs of a choppy sea, again appeared, lower at each reappearance, more weathered in tone, more desolate of color. Halfway up their sides, like the briny, high-water mark of an old dock, extended a long, horizontal white line. Its height never varied. Rough buttresses of rock jutted out from the hills, long sweeping inlets of sand covered with desert shrubs sometimes obscured its crusty trace, but the line itself never vanished. It was as if a vast sea of acid had reached up at high tide and bit deep in an indelible long stain.

"No, no, Le' Marston," Arvilla answered his questions. "Did you not listen to the words of the patrón last night when he spoke? From the Cocopahs he has the tale. Many, many years ago their fathers dwelt here by the sea. Poco-a-poco the waters left, little by little, and no man knew where. Into the mud went the water, and upon all the land stayed the white mark of the shore. Far out into the sea we go, amigo mio, but now it is but a sea of sand and no water will we have for many days."

Marston grunted and again bent his eyes to the last deposit of travertine upon the rocks. At last, down to the ancient shores of a departed beach, he was about to embark upon a voyage in a sea of geology to a land strange as the repeated tales of an ancient mariner. Lacustrine clay, alluvial deposits, crusts of salt baked hard by the sun passed under foot.

By late afternoon they reached the last appearance of the rocky terrain which rose abruptly into a cleft wall of stone. Marston, following Arvilla into the opening, suddenly pulled up his horse and stared before him.

The place was a veritable oasis of color. Vast candelabra of white yucca blossoms, those candles of our Lord, and yellow tips of the palo verde stood out against the misty splotches of smoke trees. Two desert palms like the slender masts of a docked ship, rose into the sky as if splitting by black rigid lines the wrinkled cañon walls. Desert willows and the graceful "lluvia d' oro, Señor," shower of gold, appeared with the cacti growth. He became aware of an old woman who was facing them, standing in front of a rude willow shelter on a bank of the dried-up stream.

To Marston she looked like an over-ripe fig with the same flabby body and brown wrinkled skin. Only half human the old woman appeared. She seemed to have lost all definite cinctures of time and race, as if Nature had removed all traces and in their place had thrown over her a mantle of peace and solitude as definite as it was indefinable. Only God could take care of such a half-animal desert-dweller who lived in that fountainhead of all silence and desolation. Her hair, as she shook her head, swung to her shoulders like matted strands of dirty rope.

Motionless on his horse, he watched Arvilla walk up to the old woman who calmly stared at her slow approach. Then, at a gesture from Arvilla, he dismounted and tied the horses. The old woman, he understood, was an Indian, part Cocopah, part Mexican maybe, and in return for a bit of canned food and a drink of fresh water would let them sleep within her "wickiup," as Arvilla called the willow shelter.

Again in the shade and feeling the fragrant sense of vegetation, Marston's spirits rose. He removed the packs and spread out their contents on the ground. He turned the two horses and the burro loose, after hobbling, to pick up their own meals. He dug a hole in the shadows of the trees which after a time filled with muddy water, bitter in taste but cooling to his sun-blistered skin. To these preparations Arvilla and the old woman paid no heed. Silent they both sat, looking on with the dull apathy of old women beyond reach of interest in common things. Marston curled up against the butt of one of the palms.

It was already dark when Marston raised his head. He peered down the cañon, past the dark frames of the two palms, and out over the darkness. Nothing met his eye. The world was all shadows, a softened panorama of gray and black. There was no color, no light, no sound. The unbroken solitude of night had again rolled in upon his senses.

Behind him a twig snapped, and he turned his head. The burro was noisily ambling around the cañon. Farther away there was a faint glow in front of the old woman's wickiup. The fire and companionship seemed suddenly good. He raised his voice and called loudly, "Arvilla!"

There was no answer. He rose stiffly and strode toward the fire. Seated to one side of the tiny blaze was the old figwoman pounding something in a crucible of volcanic rock. Arvilla was off to one side fumbling among the spread contents of the pack. Neither appeared to look up at his approach.

"Here, let me help. I'll do it." Marston took the molcajete and began grinding the salt and meal and chile. The old woman, without resentment, dropped her withered hands in her lap and watched with never a flicker of her pale yellow eyes, unseeing to the appearance as the eyes of a hawk.

When Arvilla walked into the light, he set down the crucible. The old woman stretched out an arm, placed it again in her lap, and as if she had never been interrupted, continued to grind like an old witch mixing an infernal brew of the desert. A long string of her hair swung from her shoulder and dipped every few moments into the mixture in the molcajete.

They ate slowly. Lee Marston picked at his food, more aware of the flickering shadows upon the door of the shelter and the presence of the two women. The old woman ate ravenously, her gnarled hands traveling in an endless chain between the pot and her mouth. She stole slyly from the sweet water canteen, but on the morrow, Marston thought, she would be back to her desert fare.

Arvilla flung a last scrap over her shoulder to the horses and leaned back with one of her ever-present black cigarettes. Seeing Marston's gaze she plucked another from her shirt pocket and tossed it toward him. The movement sent a quick flash of the firelight into the surrounding darkness. The old woman saw the reflection. Her yellow eyes fastened themselves like two fangs on Arvilla's smooth wrist.

Marston suddenly remembered the bracelet he had seen about Arvilla's wrist. El amuleto, the charm which Horne had given her, beaten in the likeness of a lizard whose flaked tail was wrapped round her wrist and whose head was the face of a Mexican dancing girl.

The old woman reached suddenly forward, drew Arvilla's arm to her lap, and gazed steadily at the ornament. He heard a guttural burst of words he could not understand, and listened to Arvilla's quiet reply.

"She want to know if across the desert where we go is the land of the Lizard Woman," Arvilla told him. "I tell her sí, Señor. No es verdad?"

The old woman was slowly nodding her head. The twisted hair tied at one end swung from side to side like the strokes of a pendulum of fate brewed from her own witch pot.

"She say, Señor, that we should not go to the land of the Lizard Woman. That it is a land not for God, not for us, or for any living thing. That it is of hers only, who made the land for God. Le' Marston, the words are true. From her fathers, the Indians of the desert, she has the tale."

Lee Marston looked at Arvilla inert on the ground beside him, resting her head against a saddle. He stretched out his own feet and moved toward her.

"Aren't we going on?" he asked.

"Chispas!" she hissed, "of course we go. Do you not go to meet the Señor Horne who waits for us? Are you afraid, Señor?" she taunted him. "We have not started yet. Do you turn back de la mañana?"

Marston looked down at her in surprise. A sharp ring of determination filled her voice. Her face was set in a mask of stern lines. She seemed the very embodiment of all those tormenting doubts that possessed him. She spoke again as though she had guessed his thoughts.

"Never can you go back, Señor. By the words of my own fathers, I swear it! " Her face grew more gentle, smoothed out to his perplexed gaze. "Are you not going with me, amigo? With your little black box are you not going to melt the rocks and say, 'This is gold, this is silver, this is cobre de las rocas?' Gold, Señor Le' Marston. Gold! Great lumps of it you will have!"

She turned to the woman, speaking in a jargon of Mexican and Indian words, and innumerable gestures. She pointed to herself and to Marston, passing the bracelet before them both. At that gesture Marston again felt a recurrent rush of protective feeling, as if they two were bound within the circle of an old legend.

"El amuleto, a charm of the gold of the land of the Lizard Woman. Always will it protect us from evil. And is he not waiting, always waiting, the Rabbit-Man who said as he gave it to me that of hers all things must return? Sí, Señor, we will reach the Señor Horne."

Even as she talked, a last stick of greasewood burned in two, fell into the embers. A series of sparks ascended regretfully into the dark mass of the heavy sky, soared past the bunched tops of the tall palms, and vanished into the smothering blackness. For an instant the vague pictures of Marston's childhood fancies leapt to his mind, indissoluble with the domain of the Lizard Woman to which he was now on his way. The phrase appeared to his eyes as did the bracelet upon Arvilla's brown wrist, glowing in the dying flicker of the fire. "The Plains of the Lost." A quiver passed over him. He knew he was already on their vast stretches, lost to the world he had always known. Lost forever from the sweet essence of light and sound which even now, far removed, was floating up to that white, upstairs porch of La Casa Blanca where once had danced with swinging breast and swift legs, Arvilla, a percentage girl.

✳ VIII ✳

THE WARM WIND moved gently, persistently. Its slow movement had no beginning, no end. As within a vast circular chaos it traveled with the hopeless insistence of imprisonment. The palms made no noise as they bent slightly at the approach of the warm breeze and straightened back without protest. All was black. The night seemed to roll like a heavy mist from off the flat sea of land, swirling in an enveloping, deep shadow up the short arroyo. At each wave the last flames of the fire flickered wildly, smothered out.

The old woman, as if drawn by brush and ink, sat against the dying flare of the embers. She was staring across the faint splotch of light which lay at her feet. Arvilla, head propped against a saddle bag, was lost in a dim reverie. As if she were thinking of the camp fires of other nights long swept away, the firesides at which she had sat with another man far out on the sea of land which enveloped them by its dark surrounding miles. Perhaps he was there now, waiting for her, waiting beyond the Plains of the Lost, over the Mountains of Fire, far even as the dread land of the old legend. Alone, beside a tiny fire, waiting silently, waiting for a moving spot to come toward him with the dawn. To tell him at last that what he had was gold; great flakes of it, lumps of gold to shake at the silent hills around him, the barren sea which mocked him by its echoing silence.

Lee Marston turned sleepily to his side and raised his eyes from his curved arm. His gaze moved swiftly up her lean brown wrist on which was fastened the gold bracelet, caressed the soft curve of her arm. The collar of her shirt was unbuttoned. He could see the soft rise of her throat straight as the pillars of the palms, warm as the firelight which gave a rosy sheen to the light tan of her skin. The Madonna-like expression filled him with a rush of protection. His eyes smoothed her lashes, stroked her cheeks. He felt, unconscious of the actual thought, that he had never been without her. Sleepily, he knew it was pleasant to lie and watch her face, to close his eyes and watch its features leap into his vision from the darkness. He wondered if her lips were warm, how soft.

The old woman rose to her feet and kicked at the full red embers. Arvilla raised her head. "Es de noche, Le' Marston," she announced, patting him on the shoulder. "It is night and time for bed, Señor. We leave early."

The woman, dipping a small branch of greasewood in the fire, held the ember at the open doorway of the wickiup and motioned inside to the far corner where lay a pile of crumpled blankets. Marston sat up. All thoughts of rest were gone. He was to sleep beside Arvilla. The thought overwhelmed him completely. Never, since the last night on the porch of La Casa Blanca, had he seemed to know Arvilla. She had changed. There was nothing coquettish about her now, no indecision, no pleading. She was a woman whose very silence was compelling. And now, in that one simply given statement, all the gulf between them was removed completely. Again he had that vision of Arvilla as his wife, a shadowy accompanying form, for the instant without appeal.

He looked up. Arvilla as a dancing girl, a percentage girl, forever slipped away as a dream which would never come again; and with her he could feel leave something else, something he had never felt before. And he knew, knew beyond all doubt, beyond the rise and fall of his easily encaptured fancies, that always for him Arvilla would be as now, kneeling beside him, her face tender as a brown Madonna.

Her hand was on his shoulder. She was talking a torrent of soft Spanish. With her finger she was inscribing them both within the hollow circle of the bracelet she held out to the old woman. "El amuleto, a charm to guide us where we must go. See how the tail of the Lizard Woman will hold us? Are we not two together then, who will go to the Land of the Lizard Woman?"

The Indian shrugged her shoulders. Her face, broken by a mass of wrinkles, brown and rough as her own earthen tinajas, was expressionless. She tossed the fluttering torch upon the ground and crushed it out between her feet. It was suddenly dark. The moon was shining like silver on a far-off strand of white. Marston heard her fling herself in a corner of the hut, heard her feet threshing about for comfort.

Arvilla in her matter of fact way was pegging the burro and hobbling the two roans. He would have liked to lie out beside the fire, seeing the moon almost within reach overhead, and feeling the warmth of Arvilla's shoulder beside his. But instead, he passed into the wickiup, lowered himself to the pile of crumpled blankets, and lay wide-eyed, tensed as if ready to leap for the open door. His eyes after a time grew accustomed to the darkness. He could make out the trodden earthen floor and the humped figure of the woman lying in the opposite corner. Above him little misty streams of moonlight filtered through the interlacing of the willow branches, played slowly about the hard, smooth floor, and raced over the blankets whenever the breeze swelled up the arroyo to ruffle the dried leaves.

The face of Arvilla leaped into his mind, drew coquettishly away. He could have drawn every line of her smooth face. He listened for her footsteps. To himself he cursed every move of the body in the corner. What could have happened to Arvilla? How sad she had seemed. As if she were blaming herself for leading him into this trip. He felt again a sweeping urge to protect her, to shelter her from every hardship. All the mystery, all the tales and legends which had filled his mind were gone. There remained only Arvilla.

A step sounded outside. The door of the wickiup was suddenly dark. Lee Marston lay quiet. His heart was throbbing painfully; his throat was dry. He could have shouted, "Arvilla! Oh, Arvilla!" but he lay quiet. She came in silently, feeling along in the darkness for the pile of blankets, for the far corner to which the curving willow withes led her groping fingers. Her hand suddenly touched Lee Marston. Her palm was laid on his bare throat in the darkness. A great throb rose to press against her fingers. Her touch was exquisite. She removed her hand immediately, finding him already stretched out on the blankets. He heard her soft ejaculation.

Lee Marston was in an ecstasy of bewilderment. The throb of his senses left him inarticulate. He heard her boots drop to the ground. She stood up beside his outstretched body, and he heard the faint rustle of her garments as she unbuttoned her shirt and loosened her clothes for sleeping. Lying quiet on the blankets he saw patches of her outlined in the splotches of moonlight which dropped through the tatters of the roof. A beam, light as a feather, fell on her face, showed her cheeks as a white patch in which her wide brown eyes rippled like a deep sink. Her throat where it met her breast was a pale splotch of snow, light and fluffy, fresh-fallen, as though unsoiled. She dropped down beside him and yawned sleepily. "Buenas noches, mi vaquero," came her words, easily, softly in old Spanish.

Marston breathed deeply. He did not answer. As he closed his eyes, he seemed to feel the weight of her glance resting on his face. He wanted to stretch out his hand; he trembled at the thought. He wanted to cry out, to tell her all things which oppressed him, to cry, "Arvilla, you are beautiful! Arvilla, hold me in your brown arms. Never, Arvilla, let me go back to men, to cities." Forever would he go with her across the expanse which lay like the soft moonlight before his eyes.

The old woman spoke loudly, threshed about on the floor, lay quiet. A bead of perspiration gathered on his brow. He rose suddenly, paused a moment at the feet of the old woman as if he would damn her presence with a kick, and passed out of the shelter. Curled under a palm, whose fronds scraped together at long intervals, Marston lay awake, watching the visions which came on the winds of his dreams, the thoughts of his ride, the night itself which wrapped about him with the insistence of the warm fold of a brown arm.

The Desert

DANE'S VOICE CEASED for the moment and we could hear his hand scraping over the table for his glass. Darkness had settled slowly, removing in its heavy folds the dusky porch from the light within. From where we sat Marston stood out half-revealed, a figure dim to eyes and mind. About him hovered the Chinese, faithful as a yellow shadow. And as Dane turned to take up the tale, a peak of bare rock, turned to a monstrous shadow of the night, drew in from the west and south. Like a vast sounding board, the echo of a man's thoughts to himself, it seemed to reflect his voice to us until, quiet at his words, we saw again that dim figure across the floor.

I'm almost afraid (went on Dane) to start you with Marston as he rode off the next morning. I am afraid, and for you, who will find no "story," no romance of intrigue, in that long ride. There were none of those conventional, epic figures of red-skin and cow-boy with which this land is associated. No "story" is Marston's; but as you see him now, I want you to see him then. You must see him, for his tale is yours as it has long been mine. Just Lee Marston, a man, just as you, Ellsworth, or as you, McHenry, might with Arvilla have ridden off into that land of silent fancy.

For so, at sunrise, they moved slowly out upon the desert on which the sun, like a warm smooth blanket, lay under a blue sky. . . .

Behind them the old woman, whose hair hung like matted strands of decayed rope, watched from the doorway of her shelter. Her slow nod, and the echo of her sonorous "Vayan con

Dios," remained with Lee Marston like the stroke of a brush across an empty sky.

Marston described their first few days across the desert in a manner impossible to relate, but in a parallel particularly true in conception. He said he felt the first day as if something had taken him by the throat. The sensations were all there—the nervous twitching of his limbs, a dull ache at the back of his head, the burning of the throat, the misted vision. The desert and the sky appeared all one color, a sage-gray of unbelievable brightness. A mist overhung the world, a mist which is sensationally peculiar to the desert. For the first time he saw it, low-hanging, with great puffs of brightness which dulled the low hills far ahead of them to a long full streak of steel. And then, as though with the momentary, absorbing sight of a strangled man, Marston began to see into the desert.

Both of them suffered from the heat. There seemed to be no escape. Sweat rolled off their faces, dripped down their sides whenever a jog of the horse raised their arms. The sun blistered their backs. Marston drank again and again from the canteen and water tins. He seemed never to get enough. Arvilla, sparingly as was her manner, did likewise.

"Pobrecito!" she warned him. "You are like a child. Do you not know that to drink so much water is bad? Where will be all the water when you have so much thirst your tongue stick out for rain? See, like this, Señor."

Putting the canteen to her lips, she began to swish and gargle a mouthful of water between her teeth, spitting it back into the bag. Lee Marston, sweat running down the corners of his mouth, turned and rode on. He spread his hands on the pommel of his saddle. The veins stood out as though he had been taking violent exercise. The flesh seemed puffy, slightly inflamed. Their whole bodies were increasing their normal temperature to counteract the heat.

The two horses lathered easily. Sweat poured from their bodies and ran in little dripping streams down their withers. Dust in never-ending cusps rose at each step, stuck to their wet flanks, and dried to a dirty veneer. Their long, finely tempered legs stabbed at the sand, began to drag more slowly past each clump of bush. Twice Marston got off and gave them water. Arvilla scowled darkly as if she resented each drop.

"What's the matter; haven't we got all that water that's never been opened?" demanded Marston. "You never did like those horses, anyway. Don't you remember how you said a horse out here wasn't worth shooting? Well, look here; where would we have been without them? No place, eh? They're really two good horses we're lucky to have and we've got to take care of them. It's hard on a good horse."

He stole a look at the long-haired burro as he mounted. It was paying no attention to the water, the evident discomfort and wheezing of the two roans. It was standing as if unconscious of the pack of four small kegs of water. Its tousled hair, stuck over the long ears and sleepy eyes, reminded him of Arvilla. They were both alike. They seemed to pay no attention to anything, yet nothing of matter escaped their gaze. They were silent; they both seemed an inalienable part of that breath-taking land of discomfort about them. He himself felt like an alien and wondered if some day he too would be a part of the desert, part of that something which would draw him to a closer understanding of the nonchalant Arvilla.

They both ate but little. Arvilla for her part seemed content to chew upon the dried fruit which evidently made up the largest part of their supplies. Marston, rummaging through the packs, was surprised to notice how light they were.

"What's the matter here?" he demanded. "Wonder what's become of that little case of canned pears and peaches I brought along? Thought when we ran out of that fresh fruit they would seem pretty good, with all that juice. Damn! My throat feels like a piece of raw meat."

He dug through all the packs, the saddle pouches. Half of the things he had meant to surprise Arvilla with were gone. Arvilla puffed at her inevitable cigarette. Her urbanity bothered him.

"How do you manage to smoke when it's so damned hot it feels like I'm breathing smoke all the time, anyway? But say, where's all that stuff?"

Arvilla coolly flipped the cigarette at his feet. "At the old woman's they are, Señor. Do you return for them muy pronto?"

Marston stood amazed. At times she treated him as a child. As if she were taking *him* across the desert, protecting *him*.

"Too heavy, Le' Marston, we have a long way to go. Already do you not see the horses how their sides bounce out and fall quickly? They do not eat, Le' Marston. The pack already is too heavy for their frail backs."

Marston remained silent.

The second day he was in misery. The night before he had walked with his blanket a rod away from Arvilla and the three animals, and settled himself behind a shadowy clump of greasewood to watch the stars, to somehow still the thought of Arvilla as he remembered her the night before. He was lying as he had dropped off to sleep when Arvilla found him in the morning. His arms, swollen terribly, were thrust between his legs; he was on his side, with big wet blisters ready to pop at the first shaft of sunrise over the flat horizon. "Jesus y María!" Arvilla cried as she saw him. "You are burning!" In actual truth he was already burned, suffering acutely from overexposure to the sun the preceding day. The back of his neck, his throat, and the upper part of his breast were covered with huge blisters; and his forearms from hands to elbows had swollen to an angry red where the sun had burned too deeply to merely blister the upper layers of skin. Not a bone in his wrists was visible; he was unable to bend his arms. He was still, like a stricken animal, moving nothing but his eyes which hung on the face of Arvilla as she bent toward him.

At her command he rose to his knees, leaned over the saddle, felt her deft fingers slipping off his shirt. The breeze caressed his back. Her fingers slid over his skin, over his naked breast, patted the edges of his blistered neck. They were cool, infinitely tender. She laid her cheeks to his blistered face, crooned soft Spanish words. Their meaning he did not know, but the soft consonants, the liquid vowels and the whispered "s" sounds came to his ears like a cool stream washing over a mossy bank. "Hold still, Señor; I feex you."

The vision burst in fragments before him. A thousand knives tore into the back of his neck; he felt ragged bits of flesh dripping down his skin. He saw Arvilla in a haze of red.

"Damn you. Damn you!" he cried, and sank again to his knees with the pain. In the red mist he saw Arvilla standing knife in hand. She laid it on the ground and stroked his wet red face. "Muchacho mio," she crooned, "little boy, I do it. I cut open blisters for you. I let out hot water. I tear off skin so it don't blister again. Camote! But sweet potato, Señor, your neck was scorched in hell!"

Lee Marston stood up. The pain of the raw blisters drew perspiration until his face ran with the wet. The damned matter-of-fact way she had opened the blisters appalled him even beyond the pain. It was the thing to do and she did it. Not a moment of hesitation. The thing, trivial as it was, got on his nerves. But he seemed to sense that now there could be none of the hesitancy, the slack trivialities of living. He had learned his first lesson. He put out his swollen arms to Arvilla.

Over them Arvilla smeared a sticky pink sap. Without protest from Marston she poured it over his burned neck. It bit like salt water, drew together the raw flesh, pained terrifically.

"Sangre de dragón—blood of the dragon sap—Le' Marston. It will cure your neck, it will dry up the burned places, muchacho."

They continued; there was nothing else to do. And as the day passed, Marston found that the red sap, a strong astringent, did as she had said. The grease from a bit of meat rind absorbed the heat from his arms. The swelling went down slowly. Arvilla's shawl he wore over his shoulders, drawn up in loose folds to protect his blistered neck, too sore for him to even wear a shirt. His arms, covered by grease and cloth, hung down at his sides. Like a black-robed monk, taciturn, evil, eyes downward, he rode on. And ever as he rode, the sea of land rolled about him in undulating swells of dusty green. Heaving surges of desert brush rippled from afar, broke beside them in crests of mottled earth. Small clusters of tiny white flowers shone in the sunlight like dewdrops of the deep, and long branches of yellow sand intertwined themselves about their feet like floating stalks of kelp. Like the unhurried rise and fall of a weary boat in a trough of the sea, the two horses and the burro drifted ever onward toward the far faint rise of hills.

✳ II ✳

AND EVER AS THEY RODE, the sun lay on the desert like a warm smooth blanket under a cloudless sky. . . .

It was a blanket in whose torn ragged folds ever tripped the legs of the two horses. More and more often they tripped, and more slowly came their long strides. Arvilla jerked her roan's head up again and again, yet it fell always forward. Lee Marston dared not feed them more water; for the more often he did, so they whinnied painfully for yet another drink. The water tins were emptied; the two canteens grew lighter.

"Por Dios! You are a fool." Arvilla pointed toward the laboring burro. "See. Look! Four little barrels of water we have. No more." She shook the empty water tin swung from her saddle bag and flung it into a clump of salt brush. "Soon we must open a barrel for you to water these scarecrows. Seguro! You wish to float them per'aps? Bah!" She spit her disgust. "Make them eat like the burro. Sage will fill their bellies better than our precious water."

This Marston was unable to do. He could only watch them with a little fear growing in his heart, piercing as the thorns of the prickly pear, letting in the doubts like sword-thrusts of Spanish bayonets into the evening skies. The shaggy burro, freed each evening of its pack, shook itself like a round little dog, rolled on the ground, kicked joyously and trooped up for its daily drink. Dried potato parings, handfuls of mesquite beans, greasewood tips and what else it gathered from all the shrubs served bountifully for food.

The two horses refused such scanty desert fare. They could never learn to eat the beans of the mesquite, to browse among the cholla with the ease of a mule deer as did the burro. They had never learned the artifices by which nature protected her only plants: that the thorns of the barrel cactus hide a juicy pulp; that the rank odor of the desert sage is its only protection against destruction by bird and beast; that all accessible plant liquid is necessarily a strong emetic. They only gulped eagerly the few and fewer scraps of his own meal which Marston tossed them in despair. Standing silently, heads hanging low with staring eyes which reproached him for ever bringing them, they seemed to Lee Marston the only reminders, the disheartening, weakening links to the bright world he had left.

Little resemblance indeed did they have to the two splendid roans he had bought for Arvilla and himself. The dust and sweat had sunk deep into the glossy finish of their smooth skins. The arch of their heads was gone; they sniffed at the ground. Their legs seemed thinner and longer each day.

Yet Marston was amazed when he found the girthing web past its last tightening cinch, and the girth still too loose. In the morning they left on the ground the two saddles, bright with nickel, rich with embossed silver plates. Arvilla threw hers on the ground with a "Hola! What a load!" It was Lee Marston who looked behind, who dimly remembered the bright tan of the new leather, the two little luck pieces hid under the saddle flaps.

The world was all a haze. There was no earth, no sky, no dividing line between solidity of atmosphere and frailty of ground. There was only a mist, a great impalpable yellow fog which hung like an enveloping curtain about them, obscuring the horizon, closing about the short hump of hills, drifting like a cloud, trailing soft streamers of dust. It was a desert mist, and through it the sun shone with great splotches of brightness. Earth was in the air. Lee Marston and Arvilla could see the globules of dust, the particles of sand turning golden orange, bright yellow, gray in the sunlight like a vast shimmering curtain of changing colors. They could see the sunlight growing fainter, more delicate of color as it pierced the thick layers of dust until it glowed from afar like the ruddy reflection of a new copper coin.

The mist was on the earth. Not always did it lie like a smooth blanket. At times it spread over the sand as with a crust ready to crack at each step. Sometimes the sand was as a muddy river: and clumps of vegetation eddied slowly about, passed under their feet, drifted backward in its yellow wash. Again, it was as if they were on the rocky top of a high precipice which extended downward beyond all vision. As if to stumble was to fall forever, to be caught in the swirling mist which hovered above them like the cloud of a vengeful Jehovah.

There came a change. Barely perceptible the color of mixed gray and dusty green of the earth began to deepen. The green gray of one plant gave way to the blue green of another hardly distinguishable. The dull green of the yucca thinned out to the vivid green creosote. The long waving arms of the ocotillo appeared more frequently. A hornier underbrush thickened about them. Innumerable varieties of cactus plant came to view. By evening they were in a patch of cacti which extended on all sides as far as they could see.

"Garden of the Devil—the Devil's playground," Arvilla named it appropriately. It was a name which sounded vaguely familiar to Lee Marston. Somewhere he had heard of a vast reaching garden of thorns, miles square of cactus. Looking about him, he realized how closely the name fitted the place. Thorns scraped his boots and raked the horses' sides. Each species had its particular method of getting underfoot, refusing to be shaken off. Beds of thick-leaved prickly pear lay in the moonlight like pumpkin patches of a Halloween night. There was no riding around them. Marston cursed whole-heartedly. Arvilla swore in mumbling Spanish, guiding her roan in the lead through the slightest rifts. Round, cylinder-shaped clumps of barrel cactus stuck out their stiff-barbed thorns.

"Heh! Whoa, Arvilla!" Marston called. She dismounted and

came toward him. "Here, you jerk this out. It's in the back of my horse's leg. You know how? I'll light a match for you to see."

In the flare of the match, Arvilla prodded about the leg. She drew out her knife. Involuntarily Marston shuddered. It reminded him of his blisters which were now just beginning to dry out and heal.

"Here, Señor. Hold tight. Ahora!" The beast trumpeted and kicked weakly. The match fell from his fingers. A warm sticky mass began to run down his hand. An answering whinny came back from Arvilla's roan. Marston lit another match. Arvilla held up a long curved thorn. "Chilito, see? A very bad thorn, Le' Marston. Look, I show you."

In her palm lay a tiny fish-hook cactus. Not more than a few inches round, it was like a baby's fist, full of the thick, inch-long barbs. He threw it away. Arvilla was wrapping the horse's leg with an old shirt. Using all the few clothes of the packs, the blankets even which remained of the saddles, Marston helped her wrap the legs of the horses and the burro.

They were forever stopping to draw out the bristling joints of cholla barbs from the legs of the horses. Innumerable thorns stuck into the wrapped layers of cloth and scratched into the flesh at each step. Ugly clumps of the cholla, the branching antlers of the deer-horn cactus, rose to the height of the horses like misshapen spirits of the night. Their mailed hands grasped at their clothes, their thorny arms scratched their legs, and drew blood from the unprotected sides of the two animals. At intervals, far off, the weird-angled arms of a lone Joshua tree stood at pained attention; an occasional saguaro, like a dead stump, loomed up its tall column and gave the sound of sleepy chirping of cactus wrens, or the sight of its desert elf-owls flapping from one hole to another in its honeycombed sides.

Marston thought they would never emerge from the vast reaching beds. He was amazed that in all the world there could be so many thorns and hooks and spikes and barbs. There was not a leaf of vegetation about him which did not bristle at approach, bare fangs worse than those of any animal. Every inch of vegetation exposed was covered with a repellent growth which tore with a savage rip or stuck deeply like a hair embedded in soft flesh. The leaves were bladed like knives. There were names for cacti he could not even see as Arvilla pointed them out: bushes of cat-claws, barrel cactus, fish-hook cactus, a cactus for every name he could think of, a resemblance to every object he could name. In the pale moonlight the earth was a far-reaching bed of thorns, farther than the jagged horizon which tore at his eyes like a tangled mass of barbed wire, far as the pale reflection of the moon, a bristling corn cake which began to glow through the forest of thorns.

Marston's horse was limping badly. Weak and slow as it had been, it now was making almost no progress. He slid off, threw the reins forward and began to lead it, picking his way carefully. Several rods away Arvilla was doing likewise. Behind her, as though browsing with utmost unconcern for thorns, walked the small burro with most of the pack. Once Marston stopped to examine the roan's leg. In the light of the match he could make out the swelling fore-hock through the wrapped cloth and see the clotted blood from Arvilla's determined cut. The tendons seemed to be knotting; the limp became more apparent.

It was long after midnight before they began to emerge from the cactus beds. For an hour after they were free, they picked cactus needles, catclaws, and thorns of every size from the legs of the horses and the burro. Above the wrapped layers of cloth, the legs of the beasts were raked and bleeding. Their own clothes were torn, their boots scratched and ripped from the cactus growth and from their own search to find the long needles, fine as hair, which had pierced the soft leather without trace.

45

TOWARDS EVENING of the fourth day they entered the rise of hills.
The hills, as Marston had known, were not the cool covered
folds he had seen wrapped over the edge of the desert. They were
brown and wrinkled as by a master hand which, after crum-
pling, had tossed them aside in disdain. Each fold was dry as the
parchment of a Cocopah's old hand, and held a burning dry
heat which made their skins pimple at its intensity.

Marston's roan was in bad shape. Since sunrise he had led it
carefully, slowing his pace to allow for the drag of the swelling
leg. The weary forced breathing of the tortured horse and the
scrape of the dragging hoof behind him were sickening. He felt
the pull at the lead-rope as if it were tied with his own heart
strings.

Arvilla was impatient. "Andele, Vd.! Come on! Three hours
to make the hills and already the sun sets. All night in the Devil's
Garden and now a day for nothing. Every day is water, Señor. Is
your mind blind?"

"The horse, Arvilla, I've got to wait for my horse. Look at
him. I think his leg is poisoned, the way it's swelling. Are you
sure you didn't cut too deep? We've got four barrels of water not
even opened yet. Wait, Arvilla, wait for my horse."

"That horse! Caray! All the time horses! They drink all the
water; they starve because they will not eat. What I say, eh? A
horse is no good here, only a burro. Leave it, ride on my horse,
Señor."

"I can't leave my horse, Arvilla. Wait and we'll rest in the
hills. Then it will be all right again and perhaps you can find
water there."

The horses must have known they were coming to water, for
they raised their heads and sniffed eagerly at each step until
prodded on. On the farther rim of the hills they made camp. It
was sunset, and the great gray mist of evening hung low, far out
over the flat expanse below. On each side, the cañon walls, like
the sides of an adobe oven, were crumbling with erosion by wind

and sand and turned to a dull drab brown, dark with the tan of years. Marston stared stupidly down at his feet.

"Bien, Le' Marston! Pick it up. What you think you see? Only pieces of old wood which will burn when the sun sets. Has the sun made you sick?"

Marston bent and gathered in his arms the scattered pieces of what might have been an old wagon. Scraps of wood and iron lay half buried, sticking out from the sand, and rotting in the sun.

"Why, Arvilla," he murmured, more to himself than to her, "somebody else has been here. Where—I wonder where they went. Do you think—wouldn't it be awful to—die, just die out here? Why," the thought suddenly struck him, "there wouldn't be anybody who ever knew it. Just come out here and never go back."

Arvilla looked at him curiously and her face assumed a strange tone. "Here, Señor, bring me that wood! You try to make fun with me? No tiene razon? Have you no mind? We must dig for water."

Marston straightened at her command, dropped his armload of debris, and began to unstrap the burro. Arvilla stood watching him. Her face, dark and smooth in the last yellow flare of day, seemed to hold the bewildered daze of a woman with a small boy in her arms. It was expressionless, strong in contour, immutable; as though not until then had she sensed in him other than the same desire for gold that filled her own thoughts. She walked to where Marston was unloading the pack, and put her arm across his shoulders. He turned suddenly and reached around her waist.

"Le' Marston," she spoke softly, "you are good to me. You work for me, you take care of the packs, you take care of the horses, and you not afraid to go with me. You not go back now?"

He brushed the sweat from his eyes and held her in both arms. Her body was limp against his, warm with the perspiration which soaked through the limp flannel shirt.

"Why, of course, Arvilla. I'm going with you all the way. You didn't think I was afraid of anything, did you, or that I'd leave you here all alone? You'd get lost."

Arvilla smoothed his cheek. "Is your head hot, amigo mio? Do you feel bad; you like to rest and have drink?"

Marston looked down at her slowly; looked deep into her shadowy eyes as though to find mirrored within her the echo of his own new-found resolve. Then he pushed her away.

"Here, you show me where to dig and I'll get busy before it's too dark. We don't really need the water with these kegs still full, but it can be used tonight. And listen to those horses making a racket for a drink."

He got out a short-handled spade and followed Arvilla to a small rocky basin. Surrounded by both horses and the burro, he dug deep, dug until he was bathed in perspiration. The horses neighed again and again. About the hole Arvilla stuck a layer of panama straw to keep the sides from caving in. No water rose. Arvilla picked another deep rocky basin filled with sand which she said would surely hold rain water once the sand was removed. This was repeated. Time and time again they dug out the center of the rock tinajas in the hope of finding water. But there was no water.

They gave up at last and Arvilla opened a keg of water. Hurriedly she opened the other three. They were small wooden kegs in which had been kept year-old bock beer from the bar of La Mantilla. Two of them were unfit for use. The salty caked brine and a fungus yet remained. Not an animal would touch it.

Arvilla forgot to swear. Marston stared stupidly. The thing sent little shivers up his back. He glanced at Arvilla and knew she would have run a knife through the bar boy of La Mantilla who had assured her the kegs were clean and filled with fresh water.

With only two kegs of water remaining, there was but one thing to do. Pegging the burro, they left the horses unhobbled and knew that at daybreak they would be retracing their steps to the nearest water hole.

The shadows and the flickering of the flames that night on the wrinkled cañon walls reassured them by the life of their tortuous writhings. They should miss the horses but little, slow and weak as they were, and the burro was proving a blessing.

The flames died. Night with all its royal serenity enveloped them in a mantle of silence. The mist and the darkness inter-mingled, were weighted by the smothering haze of heat and drifted upon them with the same ponderous presence of the rock cliffs. All the world, all that invisible lift of spirit which is the intangible presence of humanity, had drifted far away, back to the shores wherein lay like a dreamland of hushed words and faces of memory, the things which gave them life.

The land, the vast sea of solitude, beat upon their senses like the silence of painted waves. They were adrift on a pictured mist, boundless, unfathomable, containing no limit of time or thought. As if they two alone watched from afar the dying reflec-tion of their own unutterable thoughts struggling upon the black wall of a world beyond their comprehension. And then, as the stars fell out of what seemed a huge black box whose lid was suddenly snapped open, the voices of the desert burst out in a great clamor which died and blended with the song of earth and stars. The eternal voice of solitude which would forever cry in their ears. The weird cry of a lone coyote was the only discordant note, and it seemed to express the futility of the song itself.

At Marston's side lay Arvilla, stretched on a blanket with her crumpled shawl for a pillow; For the first time since they left, he thought in a haze, they were at last alone. The thought awakened him, drew his mind from the weird drooping reflec-tion of the flames. From out the flames came Arvilla's quiet smooth face, the dancing girl with the Madonna-like face he had seen first so many nights ago. The face, now tender, glowed as it had when she eased his blisters, stroked his swollen arms. All the thoughts he had felt take possession of him in the old woman's wickiup again flowed into his mind with gathering strength. They were alone. Too alone; there was no comparison. There was nothing. Only the movement of the stars in a quietude so deep, so vast, that he felt he could almost hear the dull grating of the universe turning on its hinges.

Occasionally he heard the muffled thud of the hobbled burro. He turned his head toward Arvilla. The sight of the bundle of her gave Lee Marston a steadiness he had felt but seldom. At the time it banished all doubts and fears; he knew an inflexible resolve to lead her safely into the valley of mystery, within the realm of the Lizard Woman whose symbol glistened on her wrist in the soft rosy flare of the fire.

The firelight played on her bared legs, the curved legs of a dancer, ran up and down her outstretched arm. As they did each night, they had taken off their shirts to feel the breeze, to cool the perspiration from their chafed bodies. Marston could feel the hot breeze smoothing his own flesh, sucking at the welts of the dried blisters. He thought of Arvilla's cool, caressing touch, the unblemished fragrance of her brown skin. In the red glow of the fire he could see little shadow hands softly caressing her cheeks, playing about her arms, dipping under the limp folds of the old black shawl thrown over her breast.

A little dribble of sweat rolled down his bare arms as he raised his head. The rough scratch of the blanket as he moved toward her filled him with an ecstasy of surprise. He sank down on his back; felt the heat lie on his body like a weight never to be lifted. Arvilla sighed gently and turned on her side facing him. He could feel the warmth of her breath on his wet shoulder. His fingers in the shawl seemed grasped as in a cobweb woven by a hand from whose power he knew he would never escape. Through the shawl his fingers felt the curve of her soft body, the chance contact with her warm moist breast. His hand rose lightly, fell easily at her each long breath. He felt the quiet ripple of her torso, smooth as the muscles of a toreador. Slowly he drew the shawl to the ground. And unresisting, Arvilla lay quiet, her nude body gold as sand in the sun.

A cantina-woman, Arvilla at La Casa Blanca had known many men. Creature of the midnight alleys, all the lewd love of those grim courts behind the bars was to her without mystery and without shame. Love to her, as to the others, carried no significance beyond the physical aspects of a chance meeting and quicker parting. Only the coins, all those coins which to her had meant this return to the desert, remained as stamps from the same die of repeated love. What she must have been to innumerable others and to the prospector Horne, Lee Marston gave no thought. That she had been desired by many simply raised his own pride of possession. He was in the first sweeping current of a power which forever transcends all limits of time and space, which beyond all understanding gives to a woman something beyond even her own unfathomable gift of comprehension.

As though in sleep, a slow enigmatic smile unsuggestive of any mirth and with all the fullness of desire, opened her full lips. Almost lazily, with a tantalizing slowness in the graceful indolent motion, she laid back her arms to either side. A slight tremor as if rising tide of anticipation gently undulated through her body. Her breast swelled.

Something scraped against Marston's leg. A dull smooth object, the leather coin pad strapped above her bare knee. Marston bent down to unfasten the strap and buried his face in her breast. Then suddenly he had her in his arms. He raised his head. She was awake and in her wet brown eyes he could see the reflection of two stars. . . .

Through the soft pressure of her warm body the ceaseless throb of the earth seemed to transmit itself to his trembling arms. The restless stirring of the night wind and the slow movement of the almost indiscernible clouds, like the thoughts of Heaven, filled his consciousness.

And through all the ecstasy of the night was woven a thread of the desert itself—unwavering, indomitable, restrained.

✳ IV ✳

MORNING CREPT UPON THEM silently with hanging eyes, as though ashamed at the intrusion upon a man's awakening. The weird greenish gold of the hour before dawn wrapped around Lee Marston and seemed to carry him with the hazy forcefulness of a bad dream from the sweet reality of forgetfulness to the unreality of a world which grew brighter to his sleepy eyes, uncomfortably warm under his bent head. He opened his eyes.

Arvilla, raised on one arm beside him, was staring quietly toward the east from whence came pouring the first rays of the sun like a great yellow wash to their feet. She appeared forgetful of all else. She seemed not to notice the stirring of Marston beside her, to hear his simple greeting, "Arvilla," to catch all the blind adoration in his voice, the first unquestioning love so freely bestowed. She was staring before her, and it was as if her eyes were piercing a mist not of light but of time; as if she were seeing another camp fire, another man; as if in the distance she saw the end of a journey, knew that for her at the last, as for all, must be but one path and no turning. She raised her arm.

Lee Marston, at her shoulder, knew without words that it was their destination pinned to the horizon to which she pointed. A long convex curve of blue, like the upturned edge of a flat world, fluttered in the light of early morning. The black spot which seemed soft against the cold blue, Arvilla designated as the very point.

"The Mountains of Fire, Le' Marston. Even the rocks there are of fire. Only where the notch is can we go up their steep sides. See how black it is? Everything there is burned already. It is the land of the Lizard Woman, Señor. Are you not afraid?"

Marston rose to his knees. He took her head between his hands, looked into her face, smoothed back her hair. And in his eyes was a light brighter than the sunlight spreading swiftly over the sands.

"Arvilla," he said, "no, Arvilla, I'm not afraid. I'll never leave you. But will you always stay by me, Arvilla?"

Arvilla looked queerly, appeared for the first time worried, undecided, hesitant. She said nothing and turned her head again toward the break in the cañon walls. Marston turned with her. He had begun to feel a vague uneasiness. The sight of their final destination had worked a change in Arvilla. It found an echo in Marston. There was the last range of mountains; there was the pass through which they would climb to the Land of the Lizard

Woman. And in there waiting for them was the man Horne with deposits and nuggets of gold. That was all. Yet there was something else, something which sang with a little quavering note he could not hear but whose tremolo he felt more and more often within himself. There was the legendary land, the very heart of the solitude about him; there was the man Horne. And there was Arvilla.

"Arvilla!" he cried softly.

Arvilla had swiftly risen to her feet. Marston rose to his knees and turned to the sound behind him. Arvilla's roan, which they had turned loose the night before, had not made off toward the last water hole as they had expected. There the animal was, eyes distended, tongue stretched out for water, essaying a faint whinny. Off to the side the pegged burro raised its head carelessly, began to kick up dust. Marston looked quickly around for his own horse. It was there—down.

"Dios mío These damn horses. Why they not go last night, eh? A knife in their throats will quiet this racket!"

"Arvilla!" Marston was amazed. "They had no water last night. It's been since yesterday morning that they've had a drink. Poor devils, wish we had more water."

He walked over to his own horse on the ground, stroked its lowered head, saw with a shudder the swollen outstretched leg stiff on the sand. Arvilla was arranging the pack: the two small kegs of water wrapped in canvas and old burlap, the little black box of Marston's chemicals which she handled with infinite care, the bag of dried fruit and food, the chance pieces of clothing she used for packing purposes. All else she had left scattered on the ground and Marston knew thay were to join the pieces of the old wagon in the sand.

"Say," he demanded, "you gave the burro a drink and here's yours and here's my water, but you forgot the horses. Look at the poor brute half crazy for a drink. Don't be so damned inhuman, Arvilla. You can't do that to even an animal!"

Arvilla stood looking at him insolently. A red splotch showed through the dark tan of her cheeks.

"Christ! Be damned, you are a fool!" she exploded. Marston stepped back, amazed that this was Arvilla of the night before.

"Anoche, you get white liver like a sick American. You say, 'Arvilla, Oh Arvilla,' like an old woman, when these damn horse stick out tongue for water. Look! Two little kegs of water! See, and where are the mountains now? Too far to be seen in the sun, eh? Madre del Diablo! Do you want to fall on the ground, to stick out your tongue and say, 'Arvilla,' and mix your bones with the sand? What you come for, eh? To bring box for the Señor Horne. Sí, sure! The horses are dead, Le' Marston. No horse can cross the desert I tell you long ago, yet you give out water to two dead horses! Bah! No more water they get. Sabe?"

Marston stood silent. With an angry heave Arvilla swung the pack across the back of the horse. "That's the horse, Arvilla," Marston muttered like a reproved schoolboy.

Arvilla's teeth gleamed in the sun. She grabbed the small pocket canteen, tore off the top, and flung its small contents on the outstretched nose of the horse which lapped eagerly at the wet drops and whinnied for more.

"Jesu! Sí, a drink for a dead horse. You will see what it costs, Señor. For why should the pack be carried by a live burro when we have a dead horse? Aquí, lend a hand. We hang these water kegs across the shoulders out of the way as we ride."

Marston did as he was directed. He was sullen, carried a be-damned-to-you-it's-all-your-affair look about him as he strapped the two kegs across the shoulders of the horse and tied down the pack. He rode in front, Arvilla behind him, well crowded to the rump. Behind them, without a leadrope, followed the burro, freed of its pack and unburdened in any way. Lee Marston said nothing as the horse staggered off. The broken débris of the wagon sticking out of the sand told him more plainly than even Arvilla that to conserve strength and water was absolutely essential. He kept twisting around. The hoarse shrieks, the faint trumpets of his own horse sounded in his ears. He could feel the efforts of the horse under them to answer. The poor brute was attempting to turn, too heavily burdened to do other than wobble from side to side. Arvilla beat it on. Marston faintly argued, grew insistent, declared his intention of going back to the horse. Arvilla slid from the rump.

"I go. I see if horse is strong to live, Señor. You wait, Le' Marston."

She turned from sight behind the brown bare walls, remained long, and came back slowly.

"Well?"

"I go to horse. I help him to feet—a very big job. The horse he grow strong. On three legs he jump around many times and gave a great breath of air. And I think 'thees horse will go with us for Le' Marston.' But then, quite strangely, Señor, he fall down in a heap of hair and bones which rattled on the sand and lay still. And I knew that he was not strong to live but strong to die."

Throughout the day Lee Marston saw the faint smile which was on her face as she remounted. Time after time its mocking features rose before him. He felt at times she was laughing behind him. And then in the intense heat and the brightness all things faded. They were again in the grip of a sucking current of sand which drew them slowly forward.

Through all the days Marston had felt adrift in a flat sea of immeasurable extension, level, unchanging, colored only by the thoughts which drifted through his mind like the shadows of the clouds over the plains. Now, for no particular reason, he felt a perceptible change. There was no restraining his feeling. At intervals he caught himself pressing his hand against the pack before him, leaning backwards against Arvilla, as if he were going downhill. The level of the plain had changed. It was no longer flat. It was as if all the land behind him had risen until they were on a vast, tilted table-land which sloped down to the up-turned edge of the horizon. Only the faint blue mountains appeared at intervals to stop their slow descent.

The sun burned steadily. It was all about them. It was so hot that they were unconscious of its actual presence. Marston on the first day had learned its power. Now there was no part of their bodies except their hands which they left bared to the sun.

Marston rode with his sleeves pulled down over his wrists, his collar turned up and his head down, as though it was the cold from which he was trying to escape. Arvilla, on her part, was wrapped completely in the long black shawl which now seemed an integral part of her. The mountains appeared, then vanished. At times they appeared to be made of mist. They were a cloud which the bright sunlight pierced at will. Again, to Marston, they were but a hair across the sky.

He began to itch, his legs scratched. The perspiration from the horse soaked through to his legs; the hair pricked. Arvilla complained once of the same thing yet kept him on the horse; every mile that they progressed, drooping listlessly on the struggling horse, meant a saving of many steps, of much water. The horse would stop, start up again suddenly, plod on again with hanging head and steaming sides, and each time it stopped the burro would rest in their little splotch of shade. Their progress became a routine like the sway of a slow train. Marston jolted forward to the pack, backwards against the soft warm body of Arvilla. Her presence for the moment quieted him. The night seemed far away. He could remember but faintly of a time when Arvilla was not with him. And then, as the horse would stumble, sink to its knees and throw him forward against the pack, the faint smile of Arvilla again came to his mind.

Arvilla of the night was of his dreams. She held all the alluring essence of something he had all but reached the night before. Arvilla of the day was another creature. She was of the desert, hard, unfathomable, inhuman, devoid of all feeling. The more he thought of the horse the sharper grew his pangs of remorse. The reaction of the night set in. He almost hated her, abhorred the cruelty with which she drove the horse under them.

He knew what they were doing. The horse was dying. It could not possibly stand the pace. A day without water in such a sun was not possible. Arvilla was a fiend, a miser of every atom of strength. The horse was already dead; every step they could get out of it would save them one. Even the burro had been relieved of its pack. Two people and the pack. Marston shuddered.

The forced breathing of the horse grew to a low rumble. More and more often it fell to its knees. Marston slid to the ground. His face set.

Even the eyes of the horse were glassy, its tongue was swollen to a soggy mass. Marston felt sick at the sight, a faint dizzy feeling relieving for a moment the dull pain in his head. "Get off!" he commanded. All the soft adoration of his voice was gone. Arvilla slid down.

Marston looked at the horse, walked suddenly over to its rump. The rump of the horse was a black mass of dried blood. Arvilla sitting behind him had been keeping the horse going by repeated jabs with her knife whenever it slowed up. A sudden rush of feeling, all the incidents of the past day and night, crowded to his mind in a blinding haze.

"What do you mean, damn you! Christ, don't you have any sense of feeling even for a dying animal? Killing a beast off by torture worse than a devil in hell. No water, no food, and I'll be damned if you don't want to ride and laugh about it! I'd rather walk! I'm going to say something! We don't ride another step! God, that horse makes me sick. I'm going to shoot the poor beast and feel like a white man again!"

He walked to the horse and began to fumble with the straps which held the two kegs of water. Arvilla remained standing. She looked surprised beyond all words. Her face changed slowly, comprehensively. Not hard. It softened, smoothed quietly as the unruffled surface of deep water. The horse was on its knees; the pack lay on the ground.

"What did you do with my rifle case?" Marston demanded. He knew where it had been left. Arvilla came up to him quietly. There was no determination in her voice. She placed a hand almost quietly on the bent head of the laboring animal.

"Do you want me to kill the horse, Le' Marston?" It was a simple accepted statement of fact.

Lee Marston raised his eyes. Her face was gentle beyond words. She was standing, knife in hand. Swiftly, with a powerful thrust of her arm, she drove the long blade deep into the limp neck of the roan. The heaving sides quieted; the low forced breathing stopped. Quietly, with a deep sigh almost human, the roan slid forward in the sand, head outstretched, and lay still.

Marston stood bewildered. His arms hung limp. "Arvilla!" the cry came softly, "oh, Arvilla." And in his words were all the fragments of the dreams he sought so empty-handed, all the nameless cold fears of a boy at dark, all the harsh sincerity of the land which suddenly intruded into his mind and filled his heart. He dropped to his knees beside the horse. Arvilla leaped to the ground at his side, and flung her arms about him.

"Le' Marston," came her answer. "You love me, swit'art?"

Something happened. Something other than the loss of the horse. The light of day was as if it had never been. The solitude of night rushed upon them. It wrapped around them, surrounded them in an inflexible band they could not escape. They drew closer, felt it tighten their understanding, each of the other. In one flash of comprehension Marston knew Arvilla. In that one moment he sensed in her determination the mirrored dry strength of the desert, inflexible, ruthless, determinate. All the expression of her spirit overflowed into his; he understood in her the unbrooding silence which had engulfed him. And with understanding they rose to their feet and packed the burro. Slowly now they moved off, on foot over the land on which the sun lay like a warm smooth blanket under a burning sky. . . .

※ **V** ※

FROM BEHIND the sudden, momentary glow of his cigar McHenry asked lightly, "Don't we ever arrive, Dane?" And after a pause from the opposite darkness, we heard his reflective answer:

Patience—suspense; what a quarrelsome pair of hinges are these upon which a tale swings open. From you I ask but patience. Patience—for I can give you only what Marston has given me, and by hours I have heard him describe to me every movement, every relentless detail, all the countless torments of that stretch of burning days. There was no suspense, none of the significant actions which led me breathlessly from action to accomplished result in the manner of a fated move. There was nothing. Only they two, and the monotonous, the little insignificant things which make us as we are. The big things lie ahead— always ahead, like that dim, dark pass they were so soon to reach. Suspense! Good God! What else could have been more, hearing Marston as he cursed and swore and trudged on! So also was their patience. And so also was the waiting, brooding land over which they moved.

It lay like a great flat blotter before his feet, catching his eyes with its extended flats of porous sand. There was no moisture in the land, the air, or sky. The dust in his throat caught like the wispy fuzz of dry lint. Overhead, in a blinding dome of light, the sky rested on the rough broken edge of the far horizon. And there, as he watched from under his low hat brim, grew a shapeless, irregular ink splotch on the sky blotter before them. It grew to his eyes. Splotchy, ink-black, it wavered across the sky towards them, paused, circled far overhead, passed behind them. Another appeared. The world, the sky, seemed suddenly full of spots. They wavered, hung silent, seemed jerked away with terrific force. The light blinded him for a moment as he raised his eyes. A wing brushed by his head and a repulsive stench of carrion whizzed past. Somewhat hazily he saw Arvilla grab at the pack and swing quickly. The canteen, like a sling shot on a long strap, sailed after the flapping mass of feathers.

"Diablo! Los zopilotes!" Arvilla spit out venomously. The great land buzzards of Mexico. Marston stumbled after the canteen.

"Damn it," his voice was thick when he returned. "Arvilla, why don't you use your head? What do you mean? This might have spilled our water and split open the top. Hell! A drink every few hours isn't enough, let alone throwing it away. My head's about to burst open!"

Arvilla unscrewed the top, turned the canteen upside down,

and tossed it away contemptuously. "I tell you this morning you should not put water in such a small can. Where is it now? Where did it go, eh? In the desert's belly only." She patted the remaining keg on the burro's back and drew the pieces of clothes about it like a mother dressing a child. "Only in a big keg does the water stay, Señor. When will you learn that Arvilla knows, who has been on the desert before?"

Marston, head upturned, was watching the specks in the sky. They seemed like tiny flies, hanging motionless in the thin bright air. Then slowly, very surely, they began to drop in a long inclined plane of steep descent. From far away they came. Every few minutes he saw a speck, hanging still as though stuck like a blot against the sky, then slipping down to the others. They did not rise. Lee Marston suddenly thought of the two horses and knew the mission of the scavengers.

Thought of the buzzards obsessed him. He was forever looking up to watch their slow revolutions. Soon he began to count them on his fingers. Buzzards on the left hand. The vultures, distinguished by white spots under their wings, on his right. Once he heard a voice and felt himself being shaken.

"Oígame, Vd. Señor, listen to me! You must keep your head down. Do not talk. No entiendo, I do not understand your words. Here, Le' Marston, I give you another drink."

"Get out, get away! That water will all evaporate. Put on the lid, damn it, put on the lid! Hell, can't I even talk out loud? Never hear a sound, never hear a damn thing all day long. You're worse than this damned, long-eared jackass! Neither one of you says a word, just goes along, never even look where you're going. No wonder we never get there. Look how it walks, tip-toes, by God! Four legs and it tip-toes! Make it walk like a man and scuff up some dust to show it's going some place before I pick it up and put it in my pocket. Little lap-hound! I'll feed it to a buzzard if it looks around and grins at me again!"

Behind him was the scuffle of Arvilla's dragging steps. She, too, was walking in the shade of the burro. He could hear her droning voice.

"Jesu! Maria! We cannot go back. But have no fear, Señor. Walk ahead. Is not the Señor Horne waiting for our return with great heaps of gold? Do we not have a charm of the Lizard Woman to protect us? Lift up your feet, Le' Marston. Put down your head. It is too hot to rest now."

❋ VI ❋

IT WAS EVENING when Marston rose from his knees beside the keg of water.

"Say," he demanded in a voice which quavered to even his own ears, "where did all the water go in this keg? It was almost full this morning."

Arvilla stared at him calmly and patted the black box of chemicals in her arms. Marston put his hand to his throbbing head. "You been putting water on my face and head all afternoon?" he accused. "Arvilla, you know better than that. Just because I get a headache in this cursed sun is no reason for wasting all our water. Damn, my head aches. My belly feels like a furnace and yet my head is sopping wet. And there's no water to drink, just in this one keg. That damned buzzard gives me the creeps. Why don't you know what you're doing, Arvilla?"

"You make good buzzard meat, Le' Marston?" Arvilla asked gently. "Shall I keep water for myself, eh, when you feel sleepy in the sun? No, no. You come with me to take this little black box which will tell us we have much gold. Would you have me go back again for some other man? Why you have me kill horse? Would not the horse have saved us many steps that are hard to take, much water which I must put on your head? You will learn, Le' Marston, that it is Arvilla who knows these things."

She nodded her head. "Señor, soon we strike water hole maybe. Perhaps no. Once we come to water. Very bad water it was. Then we can rest. But if there is no water"—She twirled the bracelet around her wrist and patted the black box—"Then, Se-

61

ñor, you will have no one to put water on your head, and perhaps the buzzards will have much meat. Sabe, Señor?"

Lee Marston lay down beside the burro. Night thickened slowly. It was suddenly too dark to distinguish the buzzards hanging above them. At his side the burro lay quiet. He lay back against its shaggy hide and felt the regular swells of the breathing beast. It was the first time he had seen the burro drop on the ground like this, content to lie all night. A star appeared suddenly above his head. He leaped to his knees but sank down again, muttering half to himself, "Thought it was one of those damned buzzards. Funny, eh? But if I ever get my fingers on that bird's throat—"

He looked across at Arvilla who was removing her clothes and spreading out the old shawl on the ground. She sat down, head bent to the little black box still clasped in her arms. Marston removed his own shirt and boots. Then he also sat and covertly watched her. Her actions and remembered words employed his mind. He found a bitter pleasure watching her. She paid him no attention. All her care and her caresses she laid upon the box in her lap as she held it in her long, brown fingers. And as he sat there tormented by fear and doubt, something of the truth came upon him. A dream raged behind his eyes. It would not let him rest. He crawled to the shawl, tore the black box from her fingers, and tossed it out upon the sand.

"Arvilla!" rang his voice. "Tell me. What are you trying to do, Arvilla? Where are we going? Leading me on just because I can assay gold with that damned box of chemicals? Who is this man Horne you think about all day long, damn his soul? Who is he, I say?"

He clasped her in his arms, lay down at her side, felt her warm hands creeping about his bare shoulders.

"Arvilla, do you love him?"

"No, no, Le' Marston, listen to me," came her answer. "Gold. How many times I tell you we go after gold. You have forgotten. You look all day into the desert where there is nothing. For I see nothing when I look after your eyes. Me—Arvilla—never do I forget. When I have gold, Señor, then will I go spit in their faces. Dios! but I hate them who have pushed me away with a laugh." Softer came her voice. "But you amigo mío, have come with me. And for you also will be gold and the love of Arvilla."

Fears of the man Horne drew slowly away, obscured by the pervading darkness. Only Arvilla beside him was real. How shadowy all memories of people were. Colorless, shapeless, they floated across his mind. Only the white light of their pale faces stood illumined for a brief instant; a voice, a brief, remembered phrase leaped from their vanishing forms. The touch of their hands was cold. Sawdust figures who came and went and touched him not. They had no breath of life, no lift of spirit, no softness of living flesh.

"Arvilla," he murmured, and again, "Arvilla, hold me and close my eyes."

Her breast was warm to his wet cheek, her breath came and went in intermittent waves through his ruffled hair, her arms were soft across his limp shoulders. A band of life, a lift of spirit, rose to meet his thoughts, stronger even than the warm pressure of her breast. Even her thoughts, her fears, seemed intermingled in the breaths which met his own. Her forcefulness, the undeniable strength and will of life wrapped about him, shut off for an instant the intrusion of the night upon his senses. He seemed immersed in a vast wave of thought, of emotion, which tore at his heart, his very breath. He buried his head in Arvilla's shoulder, relapsed in a panting sweat, and for a moment was still.

They were unable to sleep by reason of a new torment, pimply heat. Their limp figures threshed about and kicked spasmodically. A tiny flare of light leaped like a yellow star into life. Lee Marston sat up and drew toward the glare of the burning match. Arvilla lit another and they bent down to look. The inside of both his and Arvilla's legs were a mass of red, splotchy pimples, a fiery rash streaked with white scratches from their fingers.

"Damn horse," began Arvilla, thinking of the way their legs had rubbed against the sweating sides of the horse, gathering hair which chafed at each step.

Lee Marston rose to his feet. At the edge of the outspread black rebozo, wrapped in a soft scarf, his foot kicked the small box of chemicals. Arvilla had arisen during the night to bring it back to her side.

✴ VII ✴

DAY CAME. It was as though the land like an immense desert primrose opened to the sun. Suddenly. And its petals fell forward and lay flat in far-reaching miles, glistening in the light of day. Miles like the gold of a tiger lily, whose spots were clumps of greasewood, whose drifting folicles of sand were light as fresh-blown pollen, whose heart deep within the vast flower of creation stood out in a ragged edge upon the close horizon.

Before dawn, Marston and Arvilla had been on their way. Their faces were drawn with fatigue and the tormenting rash upon their legs. Every step was agony. The dust got in the sores, their trousers scratched the rash, the sweat burned like brine. The burro, limited to but one drink at the end of the day, seemed to be getting more scraggly; the movement of its muscles appeared through the long hair. Walking was an effort. The sand gripped their boots and drew upon their strength.

The desert grew deeper, gave the sense of deep water, began to roll toward them in great curving swells of sand. From off their tops came thin wisps of dust like the spray from great breakers. And in those miles of dunes Lee Marston caught in full the one unsurpassed beauty of the desert. Color! It made him dizzy. It took his imagination and made a plaything of his thoughts. The sand itself was only a dull yellow, all vegetation a drab mottled green, the sunlight only a burning glare. But into the sky poured all the colors of night and day. It was as though a vast shimmering veil of pale lilac and diluted mauve hung from the heavens, secured in the sky by the clasp of a bright red sun whose rays, reflected through miles of dust particles in the air, came down in a rain of topaz, bright yellow, and sparkling red. This flood of color deepened with the flush of early morning. Like an iridescent upheaval from the sea of sand itself, it spread in the soughs and rose on the crests of dunes in a burnished haze of heat. Then suddenly the day was upon them with all its blinding glare and as always with the faint, impalpable, lilac-tinted mist heavy as a cloud above them.

Tears streamed from their eyes; the glare made them dizzy. Chary as they were of water, they had to stop for frequent sips. It seemed as though the water melted on their parched tongues and never reached their throats. They forgot the burning of their legs. The water dwindled rapidly. Arvilla, looking out under the folds of the rebozo drawn across her face, peered intently, continually over each rise of the dunes.

Suddenly the burro raised its head. Its hoarse breath rose to a faint sound. Marston stopped and faced Arvilla. She looked at him queerly. Without warning, they knew what had happened, knew that like the horses it would drop upon the sand, jerk, and lie still. Arvilla drew out her knife to cut away the pack. Her lips drew back slightly, ugly, a great swollen mass of cracked red. She seemed the embodiment of all evil, all the harshness of the land. A pathetic shriek came through the thick, hot air. The burro, wobbling from side to side, was away, struggling over the crest of sand.

"Don de Dios!" came Arvilla's hoarse cry. "Está bien! The water hole, Señor. We have found it indeed."

Marston panted beside her and watched the burro weakly making toward the clump of mesquite. The sand ended. Small bits of salt grass appeared, clumps of desert verbena, dwarfed bits of heliotrope. There was water. Marston flung himself on the sand beside the burro, made ready to plunge his head into the refreshing water. A kick on his head cleared his sight. There was no water. The nose of the burro was extended in the sand, rooting under a rock and dry bush.

"Arvilla!" he cried. She kicked him again.

"Get up! Poco loco! Are you crazy? Get up! What you want

to find, eh? A lake, sí!" Her voice was tormenting. "Hurry! Get out the spade. I show you water."

The mesquite seemed to grow in a long thin range like the dark bristles along the burro's back. Up and down Arvilla walked. The burro had found it, covered as it was—a shelf of rock like a deep slit. It was filled with sand. Roots of mesquite, long brown arms from nowhere, curled about.

Marston took up the short spade and began the heartbreaking task of digging out the sand. Around the hole Arvilla placed her limp wicker mat to keep the sides from caving in, lashed the feet of the burro, threw it helpless on the sand, and sat down to wait. Marston sank on the ground beside her. Thought of the water made him crazy with anxiety. He seemed to feel it running down the corners of his mouth. The struggles of the burro increased; its tongue stuck out and gathered bits of sand. The hole was filling up. Marston watched it with burning eyes. Arvilla dipped out a cupful and dripped it into the burro's open mouth to stop its cries.

"See, Le' Marston, maybe you see the burro die. You too much hurry. You have sense now to wait to see if water bad?"

Marston forced himself to watch the hole slowly filling with water. Sight of the water was maddening, almost overwhelming, yet at the same time fear coursed through his mad desire. Perhaps it was a poison spring with alkaline contents or even arsenic. There was no way to boil it; there was no fuel for fire. He suddenly thought of the black box of chemicals. His hands trembled as he opened it.

Nothing was broken. The water kept rising. There were several cups, perhaps half a bucket full. He dipped out a tube. His hands trembled and it spilled to the sand, sinking out of sight almost immediately. Arvilla's red-rimmed eyes were intent upon him, subservient, devouring, devotional. The burro set up a great clamor. Dripping with sweat, he made the test. Alkaline, yes. Sodium and magnesium salts, but no arsenic.

He brushed the box aside and flung himself head forward toward the water hole. Arvilla leaped quickly and jerked him back. In a moment he was on his back and in his mouth was a wet rag, exquisitely damp to his parched lips.

✳ VIII ✳

THROUGH ALL THAT LONG TRIP Lee Marston moved like a man in a dream. For the desert was a dream. In itself it was nothing. It was like a mirror which gave nothing of itself, but which returned manifoldly all that a man might bring for its reflection. The desert was like that for Lee Marston. He was a man in a mirror; without guidance and without an end. Only Arvilla held the course with a tenacity unspeakable. Her steady gaze transfixed that dim streak on the horizon as though it were a mirage which would wither with the removal of her eyes.

Like a hair across the sky before them, the mountains assumed added importance, grew visibly. They now were like a scrawny feather on the horizon, long and limp, whose ragged edges wavered in the wind. In the pallor of dawn they were a faint, rusty brown, changing as the heat haze brightened through the day into long twisting threads of spun brass. By night they darkened to a solid ridge of blue from the rosy glare of sunset. But never, in all their colors, in all the steadiness of painted metal, in all the hazy wavering as of a long limp feather, did Arvilla lose sight of the black knot in their midst.

Slowly Lee Marston began to change. He awoke. He had to awake. Those mountains were to be an end. I think even then he began to realize to what he was coming. He was like that—nor can any man long remain aloof from his destiny. The barren dark peak on the night they left, the long shafts in the Cañon of Palms, the first brown line of hills, had all once been objectives of accomplishment. Now each lay far behind. Before them wavered the mountains in the heat with only the black pass like a door to an end. In those mountains, through that dark pass, he would reach what he had felt existed as a child, the very core of the land on which he dwelt, the last far horizon of his empty dreams. The heart of the vast solitude about them, the heart of the land like a desert rose. All Marston's thoughts centered on that far-off wedge, as though to stop at the threshold and put his hand to that latch of black was to open to sight the purpose of his life.

It was night again. The moon had risen in its dying phosphorescence of heat and cooled slowly. The solar arches dropped away. Drained of all color, the moon rolled down the zenith, pale gray, devoid of all expression, bright with an unholy filtering of light. The glimmer of a cold world stood silent behind the dull luster of a few small stars. Sweating, he turned to listen to Arvilla's soothing voice.

"Listen, Le' Marston, the words are true.

"Listen, for it is the words of the old woman who has them from her father, los Indios of the desert. It was far back in the days when there were no days. Nor were there even nights. Nada, Señor, nothing. There was no earth or sky or sea. There was nothing but a mist. This mist was like a great cloud. It was part day and part night mixed together; it was earth and sky and sea. Jesu! What a mess it was!

"Señor! Lie still on my arm. Do you not know it is night? There is no mist in your eyes. Aqui! Está bien.

"Now in this mist, as the Cocopahs say, God looked down to see the land which was made for Him to put people on, and animals in, and all manner of birds and such things. 'Verdad!' He said, 'What a mess. Muy male, it is very bad, for my eyes cannot even see the world.' So he called to the spider and said, 'Spin away this mist from my eyes that I may see the earth.'

"This, mi amigo, is what the spider did. From the mist was spun the clouds and all the waving, colored strings and ribbons that drift and blow about the moon. Great bunches and clouds of mist were also tied in balls and dropped. And as they dropped upon the hard earth the strings broke and the clouds spread apart and made great seas and little lakes on the earth.

"And as the mist which was part day and part night, and

68

earth and sky and sea, was spun from His eyes, God looked down upon the new world.

"Far up in the sky was He, Le' Marston; higher than the stars which hang above us. Qué altísimo! How high He was. And like the moon who watches us so closely, He gazed at the earth below Him. Jesu, keep down your head upon my arm! Soon it will be morning and light to your eyes. Lie quiet, Le' Marston, and listen to my voice. Am I not talking for you? En-tiende, Vd? Can you understand my words?

"What a beautiful world it was when it was so new and shiny, Señor. The sand was bright and hard as the dance floor of La Casa Blanca. The water was like the big mirror in back of La Mantilla's bar; bushes were like trees; forests were like big melon patches. There were the wide seas whose froth was like that of new beer; there were the deserts all covered with flowers soft to lie upon; there were no thorns. María! and I am sure there was no cactus, Señor. The sun was but warm; the water cold.

"But in all the world God looked down upon, He did not see her who had made the rocks and mountains and valleys for all the beasts and the trees and bushes for the birds. Finally, at the very edge of all the earth, God looked down and saw the Lizard Woman who made the world from rock. In no beautiful spot was she resting after her work. No, no, Señor. There was only the sand and the rocks which she had left over from making all the mountains of the world. About her on all sides were huge walls and mountains. There was nothing else. And on her face was a scowl for she was very tired.

"Seeing her curled upon the mountains with her tail drop-ping down into a big cañon, God leaned down and thanked her for the beautiful world she had made, saying that forever should all the earth be a home for her people of all living things who shall find the inside of the earth not too cold or its sands too hot, or its rocks too hard to lie upon.

"Here, Le' Marston! Poco tiempo, only a little time now that the night will be gone. Listen, for the heat makes my throat tired.

"But the Lizard Woman only scowled and said nothing,

which made God very angry, and He demanded that she make the rocks and sand on which she lay into a more beautiful world like the rest. At these words the Lizard Woman flung herself down on the rocks and over a great mountain and cried loudly. Her tail waving back and forth made great hills of rocks. And all the birds and animals listened to her words as she begged God to grant her for her own this little spot of mountains and sand which was left over from making the world.

"See, Le' Marston, cannot you see in the daytime the mountains where she is, the Lizard Woman; see how close they are.

"Look! Listen to what God said because He was kind and because He was very angry. 'Here you must stay in your own land and never shall it be beautiful as the world.' And He warned all the animals and all the birds, saying that never should they enter the horrible land of the Lizard Woman, for it was hers and not theirs, or even His. Nor should ever grass grow, or bushes, or trees. Not even the horny cactus, Señor. Far back in the sky He went then. Look! Beyond the two morning stars which watch us till the mañana.

"Señor Le' Marston," her breast lifted slowly as she spoke the words, "I speak truly. Arvilla who has brought you with the black box will soon show you the land of the Lizard Woman. Le' Marston, my words do not lie."

✳ IX ✳

TIME AFTER THAT came to pass with a slow-moving succession of days and nights which enveloped Marston and Arvilla in a blind intensity. Daily there appeared inverted mountains in the sky, wide oceans of blue on which appeared ships of state which sailed to their feet and disappeared into a clump of sand and wild heliotrope. Nights came to be scant respites during which he lay with arms around Arvilla, striving to follow the vague phantasmagoria appearing before his eyes. The water they had obtained from the water-hole was already half gone. Its mineral salts in their weakened condition had been dangerous, with nothing to add to it but a handful of oatmeal and sugar to counteract the irritation of the alkali. The illness went to their heads, and for a time they knew nothing but the mountains which each dawn drew closer before their eyes. Great gulps of blue mist and clouds of yellow dust. A sun like a copper disk and a moon like a silver crescent. Yes. And ever grew that legend of a forgotten land within the white heart of the desert, whose ragged boundary grew taller each day across the land on which the sun, like a warm smooth blanket, lay under a sky of brass. . . .

The heat increased until a few hours before dawn gave them their only relief. They began to travel only at night, stripping off their clothes as they walked. The hot winds even then burned their damp skins until the scratch of their clothes at morning was unbearable. All day they lay in the shadow of the burlap pieces strung from a mesquite branch. There was no rest in such heat. Time grew precious. To lie still with the mountains dancing toward them, withdrawing carelessly alert as they put forth a hand, was madness. They traveled at all hours. The nights were long as the interminably weary days which lasted eternities from dawn to sundown.

The darkness grew shallow, turned to a dirty faint lilac, a drab mist. Then it was dawn, the sunrise was of no importance, almost unnoticeable. There was color, a riot of light and heat, but it was a clash far off. Marston and Arvilla did not notice it. Their haggard faces did not brighten. The ineffable lift of spirit to meet the day was gone.

Once Marston looked up, looked long. It was twilight and the mountains at coming of the night had swiftly receded. But they were close, solidly close; the dark pass loomed toward them not an hour's travel away. The cloud shadows sloping down to their feet turned to solid, crumbling rock. Clumps of brush disappeared. Sharp flint and rough lava tore at their bursting boots.

Surely, inevitably, Arvilla had at last drawn them to that wedge of black in the mountains, to the pass into the valley, to the last day's journey where awaited Horne in the land of the Lizard Woman. In the dimming light, the mist of his own eyes, it was as though a band of black had drawn close across his vision.

"Get up!" he seemed to hear a voice from afar. "Get upon your feet, Le' Marston! The Mountains of Fire, Señor. Look while there is yet light. Open your eyes—God in Heaven, are you not alive? Look, for Christ's sake! We have come to the Land of the Lizard Woman. Señor," the voice rose to a cracked shriek, "be with me I am afraid!"

The White Heart

* I *

ABOUT AN HOUR after sunrise they reached the top. Of the exact time, I cannot be certain, but Marston said that the sun seemed like a huge red marble flipped into a net of gray. There on his hands and knees, it was as if the minute he turned his back to crawl up the acclivity, the sun rolled upon him, shrunk to the size of his fist had he strength to curl his fingers, and remained balanced upon the nape of his neck with the heat of its surface searing his skin.

At that early hour the rocks and lava seemed drawn into folds and wrinkled by the heat. Even the air seemed to have been drawn away as if by an invisible syphon and slowly was being pumped into its place a heavy, odorless, tasteless substance which surrounded them, pressed against their bodies, and seeped like a gas under the folds of their garments. Like a dry steam it gathered about their nostrils and mouths and at each gulp drew sluggishly away, refusing to be drawn into their lungs.

Behind him Marston heard the feet of the burro scrape on the slippery rock and the thump of his belly flattening against the hill, his front feet doubled under him like the arms of an old bald monk at prayer and his back legs outstretched like a rabbit's. As he turned, he saw the burro's eyes rolling up at him. Like bowls of milk with a floating piece of toast and with strawberry stains about the edges, they looked. But, as I say, they reached the top.

Lee Marston reached it first, for Arvilla behind him had been hanging to the tail of the burro. On his belly he crawled over the last crust of that black volcanic deposit. He hadn't sweat

73

a drop, you must remember, not the least bit of greasy moisture on any part of his body for two days. He seemed burning with heat. He imagined—he knew—that it was the radiating intenseness of his desire to reach the top rather than the reflected heat of the rocks which burned his breast and face. And between the jagged edge of an outcropping of ash and a three-inch cactus growth, Marston peered over and into what Arvilla had so often described as their last day's journey.

There can be no attempt to give you Marston's words. To give you his impressions is to give you himself, and you can see only through his eyes. To you as to me, truly as a confession, are given those few minutes in which a man conceived of life and baptized in human endeavors stood with God and received a soul; and gave it back again to that infinite power of all life and nature for which only God himself has name.

Let us go back to the beginning of the last four days across the desert. At that time all distance had shrunk to a flat ribbon edged with a heat-haze of white flecked with blue. The only tear in that beribboned blue string of heat-mountains, Arvilla had told him, was the wedge-shaped shadow of some prehistoric outpouring of lava which made the only accessible pass. This, then, was the steep ascent they had accomplished during the night. On each side now, in a curling somnolent haze, continued the rope of mountains around him. Like a rope of coral beads, to use his words, flung down in a broken heap because they had changed in color to a lifeless, rusty brown flaked as the skin of a rock lizard; and each bead a broken splotch of rocky boils, a sandy rash, and pimply lava crust.

Before him—and at the sight Marston felt as though he were squatting in the position of an ancient sun-worshipper, arms outstretched and fingers spread—before him and below him, perhaps two thousand feet, lay a round sea scintillating with untold waves of borax crystals and infinitesimal particles of mica, and sands of aeon-age forever unmoved by so much as a hair's breadth. Like two pebbles of agate, he felt his eyes were, at the very hour of creation, and he told me he drew back until he could barely see over the edge. Like a fly-speck on a tea-cup rim he knelt, with the mountains curving round in two outflung seeps and interlocking with fingers of shimmering heat as indistinguishable as their own outlines. And all inside this great cup of creation was the drifted, crumbled, baked potpourri of nature, whose thick sugary crust lay miles deep. All the shimmering, incandescent softness and sterile whiteness of a sea within a sea, deeper than the level of the desert floor without.

There are times in a few men's lives when the very manifestation of all Nature seeps into their souls and fills the void to completeness. And in its ebb it takes but the inconsequential pride of being, and leaves in its wreckage bits of the very core of a man's birth. Then a man cries out in a very agony of comprehension and prays for relief from his burden. So it was with Lee Marston. He rose to his feet and felt every vestige and semblance of life stripped from him. He felt the knowledge and heritage of all mankind seep and fuse itself into his soul and transmit itself to his understanding.

He could have cried aloud and his words would have followed too closely to be recognized and their context would have at once defied and admitted all religions. He threw out his arms and felt that should a brush have been placed in his fingers he could have painted the form of that transient heart of all beauty for which men have sought in vain. He was in accord with the music of the Infinite. And with that unlocking of all boundaries, all limitations, all the empty forms of that beauty which is known to man, he saw it as it was, the bare, untouched depth of all humility. And standing there alone in that immensity of creation and alone in the presence of God, he bowed his will to an omnipotent power of nature. He felt that it was as though that spot had never known the presence of a Creator. As though the very mountain seemed like a signet ring of God himself flung on that spot and preserving forever the enclosed space from creation.

It is at such times that a man in an uplift of spirit loses all conception of the present and has removed from him forever that recognition of time and space into which he has been born. Lee

Marston, then, was on the very threshold of that realm of thought in which lies stark madness. For when a man has reached that peak at which he is cognizant of nothing but himself and his god, there is no return. Marston was at that point, but held to the sanity of the present by a single thread all the more strong for its imperceptibility—the thought of Arvilla. At that crisis of his soul when God had taken him by the hand and led him to the last barrier of His handiwork beyond which he must not pass, Arvilla had sustained him by his unconscious acceptance of her being, almost as part of himself.

He closed his eyes to shut out the dazzling brightness of that white floor, and heard Arvilla behind him. She was pulling herself up over the rocks by aid of the straps round the burro. There was no imagining her presence; always with her there was something—the life of her perhaps—something always missing. She had piled several layers of the limp panama matting on her head and had them bound turban-fashion with wide strips of blue burlap, the affair on the whole, seeming to edge over the rocks like an enormous hat. The alkaline water she had poured on her head had run down her cheeks and dried, leaving deep furrows of brine and mud. Over her shoulders was pinned the old black shawl which flopped open at each step, revealing a brown shirt devoid of buttons, and an inexpressibly dirty pink camisole covering her breasts. Her eyes, always glowing, looked as if a tobacco chewer had spit twice on a brown rock.

Arvilla had seen that deep circular depression before, yet she stood silent beside him as if appalled at its sight. After a time, however, Marston became aware that her gaze was fixedly anchored across the valley, if one could so flatter that pit of white hell.

"Ah, Le' Marston, por la Madre de Dios, she is there, the Lizard Woman! Do I not speak the truth?"

The words were hoarse, wrung from cracked and bleeding lips, and they came as though from afar to Lee Marston's ears like the wash of ancient waves upon the rocks, bitter as their salt deposits. She was fingering the bracelet now slung from her neck. At her words there came back to him the story she had told him of gold, of hardship—the tale of the land of the Lizard Woman. His own cracked lips split open and he laughed. A dry, gasping laugh of a fool, laughed at the woman he loved, whose words to her were almost a whispered sacrament; laughed because they were so true! He had smiled at the tale; it was all a part of the beckoning finger of desire and romance. He laughed again, and in that sobbing laugh of his was all the immeasurable gulf of a man's utmost imagination spanned completely. Now, every word of that tale was so true it seemed coexistent with his very conception of God.

Why, she was there too plain to see for a moment. Clear across the sea of belching heat and brightness, her serpentine body lay curled around the circular rim of the enclosing mountains. The end of her scaly tail meeting her woman's face . . . the Lizard Woman who had created the world for God at His command. And then in the very throes of conception, she had flung herself down and begged Him to leave her this one spot of untouched chaos.

And Lee Marston knew that God had forever turned His back upon the one spot at which He had put to rest the embodied spirit of that power conceived of all Nature to do His bidding. And he felt flood his mind an instant recognition of the fact that to descend but one foot into that immense inclosure was to remove themselves beyond the reach of prayer.

Why Lee Marston went on when every mind-muscle revolted against commanding his body, there was no doubt. It was beyond all question of fear. That had been drained from him wholly. Nor did he continue because of the simple fact that the day would see the end of his journey, for the long approach to the valley, he knew, would be as nothing compared to its short crossing. He continued, in short, for his love of Arvilla—and this could not be explained, for to analyze a man's love for a woman is to know at once the beginning and end of all things.

The facts are these: Arvilla, whose very nature allowed no backward step, had submerged his own indecision, had led him inevitably to the last barrier, and now in a fierce eagerness of desire, was berating the beast upon the ground. His love for her, in the intenseness of this desire which he began to recognize as a recurring lust for gold, counted for nothing. It was she who had won him to the start and who now, almost without thought, was spurring him toward its end.

❋   II   ❋

THE BURRO ARVILLA had beat to its feet. Marston then, grasping the leather thong tied about its head, began to pick his way among the rocks of the descent. Behind followed Arvilla, dogged as a coyote on a sick trail. The heat was intense. It was terrific. The sun as it reached the curve of its zenith was like a tipped kettle of molten brass, and its spilled contents seemed to run down between the rocks and lie in great slow pools in the dry barrancas and arroyos. The rocks themselves were as festered sores on the mountain side, scaled as if their contents had been drawn out by the heat and rusted upon their coverings.

The burro's breath ceased to come in noisy whistles of exertion, and only its recurrently swelling sides gave evidence of breathing. Arvilla, as she washed its nostrils with water, felt no intake of air. "Madre de Dios, he bloats before our very eyes," she wailed. Removing the shawl from her shoulders she pinned it about the beast's head, wetting the parts covering the nose and eyes throughout the rest of the day. Marston, unhooking the belly bands, felt the straps were as long welts on the animal, so hot and shrunken into the skin and hair they were.

And all else beside the last water keg, the small box containing the chemicals, and an old saddle bag with their remaining food and clothes they threw upon the rocks and continued. The box brought to his mind, like a tether to a dragging past, the thought of the prospector Horne. Something grew in his mind as he remembered Arvilla's silent staring as they came over the desert. She had spoken of him rarely, yet Marston knew he was always in her mind. Each thought, recurring with the intermittent monotony of a slip on the rocks and the viscous drip of perspiration, was a new torment. Within a mile, within three thousand steps in three directions he knew it was Horne's influence which had led to this end of all things. And at the end of an interminable chain of heat soaked minutes which dangled their links across his eyes, he knew he was a futile instrument led blindly as the beast behind. Led with a little black box, a doctor for a gold cure, whose life was worth only the box. He, who had looked with awe upon his soul and wondered to find it himself, was to connect the speck of his past to the infinitude of eternity with a path drawn through all the world straight to Horne.

"Señor!" came Arvilla's faint cry. "Wait for me. Why do you hurry now? Wait for me, Le' Marston."

The sun, now glowing like an impossible fire ball, had arisen at the back of Arvilla and Lee Marston at the beginning of their descent. They therefore had the choice of two routes: to follow the enclosed semicircle of the enclosing mountains, the bottom rim of the analogous teacup; or to cut across the bottom in a direct line. Subconsciously they had ascended in a zigzagging line, working well to the south in hopes that they might keep the sun well behind the mountain walls as they completed the curve. The fallacy of this intention they at once perceived when they began to understand that their course at no time paralleled or kept time with that of the sun.

By noon, watching it creep ahead of them by degrees, they had been forced to the inevitable conclusion that they must walk directly into its rays. The prospect appalled them and they assayed a direct cut across the valley floor. Once away from the walls they were adrift on a sea of such vastness that its very desolation drew them with the same force which leaves the rocks of a shore line wavering on the horizon and diminishing in great gulps.

This impression was particularly applicable for the reason that it was in all truth the shore of an ancient sea. The sand was hard and smooth, glazed and intermixed with a white salt deposit. At points outcroppings of borax appeared. And brooding over all, the Lizard woman lay coiled with the ease of a wanton on the top of the mountain which rose from time to time like an island of opal from a sea of brass.

From the north there would appear dust devils a thousand feet high, raising their long twisting bodies high in the air and gliding with unbelievable swiftness and smoothness across the sands. The south wind, burning out like a rocket, would leave them dipping their heads and gyrating slowly, a veritable garden of serpents all in graceful obeisance to the slothful figure before them. These hot air vortices rising from contact with the heated surface gave Marston and Arvilla the utmost concern, catching them in their coils, compressing them with sucking heat constrictions, tearing their garments with rasping scales, and leaving them all but insensible to each other.

Lee Marston, with his exceptional facility for the retention of detail, watched the figure on the mountain closely. The Lizard Woman was slowly changing as they approached. He was aware of seeing the flakes of her scales turn rusty brown; the next moment the golden gleam of her flesh had become rosy as with an innate quickening of desire. And at that moment he felt the fulfillment of the dread apprehension which had so oppressed him that morning; as if before that slothful figure whose flesh gleamed with a rosy desire, he was awaiting his own condemnation.

The gradual oncoming of this red haze Marston could not, of course, account for, being as it often is, a direct assurity of snow and desert blindness. The small capillary blood veins feeding his eyes, overcome by the excessive strain, had broken and discharged their contents. These were filling the delicate tissues with blood, in no way impairing his sight, but providing for several days a dull red filter for his every gaze.

After a time they found themselves once again traveling with the rocky cliffs to their left. This alternate route offered no relief. The walls but served as a quivering heat curtain to reflect the sun back upon them. Strangely enough, but a few hundred yards away the same walls hung like a gossamer damask and in the attendant heat vibrations changed into a cool wall of beckoning blue, a blue of washed-out purple, like a diluted wine.

"Le' Marston, for the love of God, Señor, I cannot see!"

They stopped. Arvilla dropped to her knees, put her hands over her eyes to shut out the blinding glare. Marston stumbled beside her, got out a handful of matches. The flames as he lit them held no heat; they were but dull yellow flares in the sun. Under her eyes and over all her face and his own he rubbed the charcoal sticks to prevent blindness.

They stopped again. Twice they stopped to kneel in the sand to remove their shoes. Their worn boots, torn by the sharp flint and lava, were ripped open, split at all seams. Their sufferings were terrible; the red rash from dust and perspiration, the thick swelling from the heat, and finally the torn cuts and peeling of great pieces of blistered flesh from their soles. What little oil they had they rubbed in their feet. It burned like acid; each step was exquisitely wrought pain. There also, kneeling in the sand, Arvilla tore strips from her limp, wet camisole to bind round their feet. Beyond sensibility of even pain they rose to their feet, knew nothing but to go on. Speech was forgotten; there was no limp in their pace.

When the cavalcade—as that sorry mass of intermingled man, woman, and beast might be termed—again began its creep onward, like a huge centipede moving innumerable legs for every foot of advancement, the positions of the three were significantly fixed. On one side of the burro, alongside its head and clasping the halter-strap, walked Lee Marston. Across from him, both hands slipped under the belly net, struggled Arvilla. An odd trio, the blinded burro wobbling from side to side as if pulled between them from one to the other. Marston was in the lead. That was the significance; Marston himself who almost unconsciously, insensibly, was now driving them to the end. In him all indecision was forever gone; he was making plain that whoso loseth all first loseth himself. Even Arvilla, sensing the change, lolled behind weakly, head across the burro.

There is no striving to grasp the power in the woman Arvilla, on whose unconscious inflexibility of will now rested more than the life of Lee Marston. To him she was for always but a shadowy form, a one tenacity of purpose against which his own sleepy indecisiveness glowed the more fitfully. In appearance she was all breasts and legs, without hips like a boy, and she possessed an accent, Spanish and yucca-sweet as it was. Such small things, nothing in themselves, made up all Arvilla. In her there was no ingrained pride of being, no conscious possession of power. Her very force was a vagrant current from that torrent which has for ages swept man into madness. Gold!—great cakes of it!—had filled her desire to bursting, and the trickle of its dust made never-ending music to her senses. Every kiss and promise at the start had held the lure of its yellow bubbles of wealth, and every torture had been a further urge to its garnering. Lee Marston had seen it in her eyes that morning as he turned to help her to the rise. The very proximity of it had filled her veins with heat. Tenacity of purpose! Why, she had lived on the thought of gold for two days. Yet for all the wild music of her senses, something in Marston's eyes, sinister perhaps, brooding, expectant, held her back. There he was, burning red eyes in black cheeks, staring fixedly into that opalescent chasm which now began to appear at frequent intervals.

The desert! To Arvilla, it was a means to an end, a something to be endured. But to Marston it had been something else. It was there, inexplicable, unimaginatively remote, beyond all of time and place. Its simple barrenness robbed him of revolt; its unobtrusive cruelty had taken him unawares. In Arvilla's tenuous grip he had moved as though asleep. But now, seeing that coiled figure before him, he awoke and saw it as it was. The desert! Not a contradiction, no soporific, not barrenness or an empty shell. Rather was it an immortal paradox of Nature, for of all things it held the most in the untouched depth of its white heart. The figure, like an emissary of a familiar hell, drew him with a force beside which Arvilla's lust for gold was nothing. Beyond all hope of prayer, Marston felt himself led into that land which seemed, beyond doubt, to hold that one secret of all things, the solid heart of an empty dream.

Dimly realizing it was the canon to which they had been working, he raised his head and felt his gaze drawn to the figure of the Lizard Woman surmounting it. At the sight a slight tremor pervaded his limp body. Her arms were long, outstretched; they had long enclosed him, drawing him closer to her rocky breast, and he could feel the hot whispering wind of her poisonous breath.

They were entering upon a long fan-shaped wedge of silt which had poured forth from the extinct mouth of a deep cut river bed. Everywhere glittered an unbearable brightness and in all directions heat waves crawled over the sands. It was an immense sea of solitude, of geology alone. They were in the midst of a shimmering whiteness unbroken by so much as a crusting of alkali. The silt was fine as sifted flour. An intense desolation pervaded all. The very air seemed to have a substance of silver. The illusion of water in the distance was gone. Nothing remained but a blinding monotony following the sands of their footsteps and closing slowly about their heels. A bursting silence seemed to have engulfed all time.

Perspiration literally dripped from them. Marston could feel it running down his cheeks and breaking from his body until he feared that it was his flesh melting away.

A great gulp of blue mist before them slowly began to puff out like a bursting cloud. Without raising his head from where it was bent against the burro, he began to feel his feet released more quickly, and after a time to feel them grip firmer gravel. He opened his eyes. A pink giddiness spread over him and for some time he could not distinguish his surroundings. The light was too intense and the atmosphere of below sea-level was taking effect.

They had crossed the level, white floor of the valley.

✳ III ✳

THE SILENCE, which had been so intense that it seemed the living voice of creation, ceased. The burro stopped. The river bed, narrowing between two uprising walls before them, seemed filled with a vast torrent of noise unperceived by the senses. They were bewildered. They raised their heads and waited—waited for something they had never before experienced. It must have been horrible. Marston said the semblance of that exhausted, dried-out monster in repose above him seemed to awaken, to stretch out her arms in lazy welcome.

The broken silence, hanging heavy as painted billows of sound, suddenly rushed down. The noise enveloped him in a vast swirl, and eddied about them with great ripples of sound. Arvilla beside him was standing as though in stone. Another rock rolled to his feet. He became aware that he was hearing the rattle of its passage and a series of short squeals and weird shrieks which he thought were his own. A flash among the rocks caught his clearing gaze. A grotesque mass of skins and waving arms was hurrying down the cañon side. It was the prospector Horne who had seen their slow approach across the valley.

A cry came from Arvilla. Her blackened, burnt face, like that of a boulder, split into a thousand cracks. Her eyes widened; she tumbled toward him, fell heavily on the ground.

And then, like a face in a dream, appeared the features of the man Horne, el hombre conejo—the rabbit man, beyond all doubt, true as Arvilla's words to the smile. He had a long lean look like a jack rabbit's, almost as though a huge pair of hands had taken his cheeks by the flesh and jerked backward over his ears, leaving his teeth protruding. Marston, seeing him in Arvilla's arms, thought the man's head was going to drop; it was that top-heavy, with an inverted slant from the nose to the neck; a wedge driven between his shoulders. His wild greetings to Arvilla were quite unintelligible; each time he closed his mouth it looked as though the top of his head dropped like the lid of a box. His hair, what parts of it showed, looked burned and dried up. The rest was probably white.

He suddenly saw the burro. Tearing off the pack he burrowed through the contents like a gopher. Saliva dripped from his mouth as he chewed on the last bits of dried fruits; he tossed the few old clothes in the air with mad exaltation. He was on his knees when Marston stumbled up to them with those bursting, blood-shot eyes of his.

For an instant the prospector, like a wild animal, seemed immobile with fear. Then with a leap he jumped away to safety behind a rock. Marston stood still. Arvilla, scrambling to her feet, immediately took his hand and began to speak, pointing to the gutted saddle bag on the ground. The small black box brought Horne from behind the rock. He approached them warily, circled about with the box under his arm, and then reached out to stroke Marston's sleeve. A sudden wave of antipathy gripped Marston. It was stronger than that. He shook off the hand and sat down, too dizzy to stand.

Arvilla came to him immediately with the remaining water. The trickle of it down his throat, the wet cloth about his wrists made no impression. He was watching Horne's face, watching it steadily as it in turn was bent on Arvilla.

It was Arvilla, whose knees were trembling until she could hardly stand, who directed Horne to bind the pack and keg on the burro and who urged Marston upon his feet. The prospector's animal-like eyes were still on hers as they moved up the cañon leading the burro. Lee Marston followed slowly.

It seemed hours while they steadily ascended the dry arroyo between high, wide walls of rock, though the actual distance must have been extremely short. The river bed as they ascended, grew more varicolored in tone and appeared more clearly like a serpentine monster. Sand and crumpled rock formed grotesque patterns on its belly and sides. Ahead, the uprising walls seemed streaked with red and the bluegreen of an insect's wing. Behind, the shining sand reflected rocks upside down and gave back the perfect illusion of water. On each side they passed huge, baked pillars of sand. The rocks seemed smooth, delicately tinted, with the imprinted patterns of the leaves and plants of a vanished vegetation.

The ground was covered with unfamiliar colored stones which glittered in the sun. Sulphurous green stones and grayish masses streaked with flames; purple colors and bright red agate bits like birds' eyes; black lava like deep pools; bloodstone; jasper.

And now from time to time they began to catch sight of serpents and all manner of lizards: horned chuckawallas, long alligator lizards, innumerable small sand lizards scuttling among the rocks and vanishing instantly, mottled leopard lizards almost indistinguishable. Once, not an arm's length away on a level with Marston's eyes, lay a Gila monster with its pale markings of salmon pink on hard black beads as of a lady's bag. Horned toads in the oven-like shade of the rocks round Dinapate beetles, and brittle scorpions. The Land of the Lizard Woman! There could be no doubting it. Her inexorable, commanding spirit was about him. Each step he took seemed to be upon her flaked side. Each ridge of rock was a fold in her horny skin.

"Ah! Gracias a Dios!" at last came Arvilla's cry to his ears. "Thanks to God; we are here!"

There below them at a level spot on the side of the dry river gorge, Horne had awaited the return of Arvilla. It was a desolate, sorry spot; but from a fissure in the rocks trickled a small stream of water which left an alkaline ribbon on the ground before it vanished into the sand. There in a cleft of the rocks, almost too narrow to be called a cave, Horne had nursed an unconquerable will to live which had slowly changed into a hardened essence of that very desolation itself, unapproachable and unfathomable.

The burro, sensing the end of their journey, sank to its bloody knees in the first shade. The empty water keg strapped to its back burst with a hollow, echoing report as the burro flopped to its side. Arvilla, unmindful of the box in the pack, wandered to the trickle of water, discarding her clothes, and began to splash the briny water on her bare shoulders. Horne squatted eagerly beside her, running his horny hands down her wet arms, through her bedraggled hair, rubbing his whiskered cheeks across her breast, murmuring all the sharp animal sounds of a man insensible to all else. Arvilla's own face was a blank. Her body was limp and wet with the lassitude of tortured nerves which demanded instant cessation. All the fiery will, the strength of life, the grim determination which brought them across the desert was gone. She had collapsed at last. Like an old woman, she was an empty shell, resoundless of spirit. There was no twitching of her blood-clotted feet, no tension in her limbs. She lay like an empty sack.

It was the end of the rainbow trail; they had arrived for the pot of gold. Yet there was something more. Tantalizing, it hovered in Marston's mind as he collapsed to the ground. In what seemed the innermost ears of his mind, the pit of creation, the heart of the desert, cried in a great clamor, assumed a woman's voice, died in a far-away whine; and with one twitch of overworked muscles he lay still.

✳ IV ✳

IN A STUPOR of exhaustion they lay until the afternoon of the second day. Night came and went, like a black hot hand passed across tired eyes. Great heat blisters rose upon their bodies, glowed like white-hot pains, and faded as perspiration drew the poison from their blood. Day came, impressing upon Lee Marston's eyes, which saw with the dull fixity of a photographic plate, a sensation as of a revolving brightness sparkling with many flashes and colors.

He was aware of something moving about, flitting back and forth from the entrance; a desiccated shadow of a man squatting before him for long hours, mumbling and caressing the burro off to his side, floating away at each groan. From his side, Arvilla would rise for water with all the decisiveness of a somnambulist in a weird dream, wipe off face or legs with a wet hand,

and relapse again to immobility. The shadow from the doorway lay long on his face. He felt it tugging at her beside him and then they vanished, and the light lay again before him.

And then on that afternoon of the second day, Lee Marston awoke within the sterile domain of the Lizard Woman. He sensed that instantly; all else, all those weary miles, like a vast shimmering haze of heat lay like a curtain across his memory. There was no pushing it aside. The Lizard Woman!—there her scorbutic, wanton figure waited upon the rim of the mountains before him.

And when he passed a limp wet hand across his eyes and looked out, two figures were in the doorway. Arvilla, naked to the waist, was lying across Horne's lap, clutching the little black box of chemicals. He was playing with her, patting her head, rubbing her arms with those long claws of his, and rolling little pieces of rock down her neck and breast from a pile of black and yellow stones at her feet.

Lee Marston sat up.

Later, haltingly, he told me that at that moment there seemed to die within him all feeling for Arvilla. Not love for her, for the word is too trite, suggestive too much of that passion which ebbs and flows with the tide of life. With Marston, Arvilla had been the very essence of that stretch of days which had burned their passing upon him to the exclusion of all time. With the passing of this, like the sinking of an underground river in the sand, his days lay coiled round his memory in choking clumps of beads.

He stood up, tottering in a dizzy haze. Both Arvilla and Horne, whose faces glowed with the same unrestrained eagerness, and whose hands trembled as they held the gold ore, seemed far removed from his understanding. Then something penetrated his mind.

They heard his step in time. Arvilla received his kick on her shoulder with a surprised scream as she fell backwards. The pebbles flew from Horne's hands as he squealed with a wild whimper, leaped apart, and crouched trembling in the doorway.

"Le' Marston! Señor, are you mad?"

She flattened against the rock wall from sight of his face,

the black box pressed tight against her breast. Perhaps Lee Marston was mad. And perhaps he was thinking. He must have had some inkling of the truth, watching Arvilla by the nights as she stared across the desert, thinking of that box which meant more to her than all else. For the first time he saw himself in the light of day. The dream had vanished. And he stood there stripped of all those shreds of the glamor of a youth that had forever fled. For him the sun had set, and the darkness was a depth unlighted by the flickering of any dream.

Horne backed away, slipping down the cañon from rock to rock. And Marston behind him forgot that figure as though it never were. He was that absent-minded. It was that unimportant. Horne and all.

Even later, those many nights when Marston sat trying vainly to give me a reason for what happened, there was no logic in the train of events that followed. He remembered that the sun was terribly hot upon the taluses of stone as he crawled down the cañon wall, as though he were still following Horne. So he sat down a moment.

You can imagine him sitting there, head on hand, staring as though grieving, blankly, down into the dry wash. Perhaps in an hour he rose and went back to the cave. More than likely that is what happened, and a day or two later he again wandered out upon the great talus of stone. Perhaps not. He could tell me no more than I can tell you. It is of no matter; feeling was not within him. His love for Arvilla and that awareness of little things was gone. A day, two days later, a week, would have made no difference.

The thing to tell you is that something caught his gaze. A peculiar flashing in the reef of rock, crystalline in appearance. Almost before he picked it up he knew that it was gold. The undersides of all that gritty black rock were flecked with gold. One of the most perfect deposits he had ever known to exist. Washed down by the ancient river and exposed for ages for the sun to bake, the wind and sand to hide and then to uncover, and for the lizards to crawl upon. A marvelous structure he insisted, though

89

with the utmost dispassion. A side vein gorged by the river and left to fester in the heat.

The thought stunned him. He was aroused by a shout from above which echoed down the cañon with a long wail of sound, "Le-e-e Mar-s-s-ton!"

He looked backwards. Arvilla appeared, following a noisy clatter of rocks which plunged over the steep arroyo walls.

"Señor! Have you gone mad? Why do you sit here where the sun is bad for your head? Do not be angry, do not hurt the Señor Horne. Have you forgotten? He will give you gold. There are bags for us all. Come back—come back where you may tell us with your black box that we have gold. Señor! Do you not love me, Le' Marston?"

He pushed her aside. She grabbed his arm.

"Stay. Look here. See him, Señor?"

Marston looked down. Horne was crossing a flat shelf to a rough parapet of stone, above which hung two heavy blocks of black igneous rock. Looking closely, he saw that they were attached quite ingeniously with long withes and patched lengths of leather to two cross-arms of dwarfed mesquite. A central spindle was sunk in a rough hole in the flat bed of stone.

"See, Le' Marston? See where Horne has broken the rocks in his arrastra for you? Watch him as he brings you gold, who has brought Arvilla across the desert."

Horne was pushing aside the crude cross-arms fastened to the spindle. The Mexican rock-crusher was cruelly ominous, and Marston knew that the dust and broken stone he was scraping into a bag of skins were the results of anguishing days of toil. Hearing Arvilla's shout, Horne waved an arm and began the task of lifting the sack to his shoulders.

"Come with me, Señor. See how he is bringing us gold to test. Were not my words true, are not the very mountains of gold! See the great flakes in my hand. Come"—she took his arm and began to back up the hillside—"I have a fire for you, for you to test with the little black box I have guarded so closely. Do not be angry with me, Señor." Her voice lowered. "We will get gold, much gold, for you, Le' Marston, and then will we leave this land of the Lizard Woman. I have patched your boots. I have filled skins with water. For sometimes, Señor, sometimes I am afraid—"

✳ V ✳

A FIRE WAS BURNING outside the doorway of the cave. Its waves of heat mingled with that of the sun reflected from the bare rocks. Marston, with an imperturbable face, reached for the box of chemicals.

"God in Heaven, Señor, smile with your eyes. It is of you I am now afraid. Le' Marston, what has happened to you?"

She shrank back across the fire, raising her eyes to the doorway where stood Horne lowering the sack from his shoulder. His face with its receding chin, slanting forehead, and beady eyes looked furtively askance as Marston took the bag and emptied it upon the ground. Through the mass of crushed ore Marston ran his hands, selecting pieces for easy assaying. Horne crept closer, and he could feel the man watching his every movement with the tubes, trembling in every limb, tense for instant flight. When he raised his eyes, it was Horne who dropped the look.

"Ah, but he is wise," came Arvilla's anxious words, "for did you not cure the bad water for us with this box, Señor Le' Marston? Un médico de rocas, a Rock Doctor, eh, by Jesus!" She laughed nervously. "And now you give us gold, no es verdad?"

Marston was amazed at their childish eagerness. Poor ignorant fools. Not to have the confidence of their eyes, not to know that beyond the first flush of discovery lay all the problems. Yet they insisted upon a test as though it was something they could not hope to believe. All those miles to bring *him*, on whose words now rested months of hope and faith. They perturbed him, compelled his actual awareness of the hardship, the months of loneliness for the man Horne, the faith and indomitable resolve of Arvilla. Yet a dim, faint sense of power thrilled him with a

91

cruelty of restraint. Whatever he said they would believe. Now his was the will; he held them by the manipulation of his fingers.

They crowded forward with pathetic, beseeching eyes. He made a small furnace; completed his preparations. And like a priest before two penitents, Lee Marston set out his tubes and chemicals—nitric and concentrated sulphuric acid, chlorine, and some potassium cyanide. Horne's face, he saw from the corners of his eyes as he filled the tubes, seemed quivering like a noosed rabbit. Into the first of the two tubes he dropped a thin flake nicked from a piece of rock. It dropped to the glass bottom and lay still. He watched their ignorant, eager faces a moment before speaking.

"Gold is insoluble in nitric acid, but now watch it dissolve in this chlorine."

The chipped piece in the second tube, as he held it to the light of the fire, crumpled suddenly, collapsed in murk and vanished. Marston looked up at the two figures watching him with blank eyes seeing nothing but his face. Arvilla's voice broke upon his absorption with the imperious note of old.

"Where is the gold, Señor? Where is the gold of the land of the Lizard Woman, eh? I see not lumps of gold. You only melt our little pieces away in burning yellow water and pound out big brown pieces and rocks into the pan which you put into the fire to burn. Diablo! That is not gold for us to put into big bags What you do, eh? For what you come with me, Señor? Bah! Your eyes are sad, you are angry, you know nothing. You tell me you melt rocks, great rocks, and get gold, gold for us all, gold for Arvilla's mantilla when she is a muy gran señorita. Where is it? Do you lie to me, Señor?"

Her eyes, like two flames, twisted with anger. Marston only turned casually, tube in hand, to Horne, whose face was struggling for expression, little white wrinkles swiftly crossing his brown cheeks in a mask of astonishment and misery. Shrugging his body, he drew out the molten mass from the fire to cool.

"You damned ignorant old fool." His voice came slowly as he made his preparations following the scorification. "You expect me to melt the mountain side and give you snowballs to roll home?"

Horne had not moved, watching him with one eye as he knocked away the cooling slag, and then flashing a furtive glance toward Arvilla who was drawing up closer. In the center of the mass of ore lay a small button of metallic gold and silver. The separation of ever-present silver depends on the solubility of silver and the insolubility of gold in the nitric acid and in boiling concentrated sulphuric acid.

Marston then showed them how the cyanide process was carried out in large reduction mills. You know what it is. The metallic ore is treated with a solution of sodium or potassium cyanide. The dissolved metal is then precipitated from the solution to a zinc plate and then removed by dissolving the plate in acid.

And then he showed them how gold amalgamates with mercury forming a white amalgam of pasty consistency.

Arvilla crouched before the fire, held as though by some remorseless attraction. Her face expressed disbelief; her sharp eyes were distrustful. Horne was silent, bent over, wiping off the corners of his mouth with a shaking, crooked hand. Marston talked on. His voice rose and fell only with the inflection of his words, quieting them with the slow sureness of his diction though the words themselves neither could understand. There was no elation, no interest in his voice.

Describing the reactions of the acids upon the gold, he said he felt amazement only at himself for the lack of feeling at seeing how perfectly true and fine the gold emerged from his tests— a dream of perfect execution come true. There it lay, a small button of gold for all his crude work. The pure, golden heart of that forbidden solitude, the heart of the figure on the mountain above.

It was simply, after all, what he had come to do. And they believed; they had to believe. He rose and stood there stupidly, staring down at Horne and Arvilla who seemed to have forgotten his presence.

Horne, overcome completely, was on his knees. A thin stream of saliva dripped from the corners of his mouth in which he had thrust the gold button. In his hand, like a crucifix, he stared at a glass test-tube. A gibberish flow of words, all the pent-up emotions of months, came in vast throbs which shook his ragged body. He grasped at Marston's legs and began to kiss his patched boots.

Arvilla, as he turned his head, was in all probability as delirious with fatigue as with joy, for she was alternately weeping and crying, rolling on the ground, and embracing the enraptured Horne.

"Por Dios! Gold, Señores! Puro oro. We shall have buttons of gold big as our fists. Bags of oro de polvo fine as the dust at our feet. Gold for Arvilla's dresses, to put in her pockets, to throw to the dogs who gave her but dos pesos for a dance and a little love. The mountains are full of gold for us to pour in our laps. Jesu! You love me now, eh? Gold for us each! Gold for you, gold for me, and for you, Le' Marston, to be a great man, el más rico, Señor, the most rich of all Americanos! Ah, how great a señorita will all men call Arvilla, who once held her in their arms. Bah! Cochinos, pigs, dogs, filthy rats! Only you two, my brave Señores del desierto, oh, men of the desert, will I have in my arms!"

She rose, ran to Marston and passionately kissed him; kissed his arms, his shirt, his head. He threw her off and tripped her to the ground. Dispassionate, coldly aloof, he watched her roll over. Unmindful, she scraped up a heap of ore into the saddle bag which she tied to the burro with a leather hobble thong.

"For you, mi burrito," she mouthed, "for you whose legs are short and whose hair is long. Never did you fall and die, nor did your bones stick out from no eating in a big belly. Thirty pesos I give for you. Three thousand, un mil o más, I give you now, Señor Burro, for even the ground is gold!"

Over the burro she was flinging handfuls of dirt and sand scraped from off the rocky floor. Lee Marston turned from them, bewildered by their wild actions. A ray of the last sunlight of the afternoon lay like a bright yellow shadow of gold before him, lit up his cold calm face.

Like a man bereft of all emotions, and as though unutterably sad, he turned and sank against the ledge of the rise before the spring.

✳ VI ✳

EVENING HAD COME. A sunset had burst within the valley and its colors were diffusing the world. Taluses of broken stone lay heaped about him like ashes of rose leaves. The mountains were indigo, and the ridges of the river-bed carmine walls to a flow of gold. Slowly the chrome yellow slipped into orange and then into a deep plum color. Blue of every conceivable shade and mixture seeped into the far-off sinks and drew the indigo in deep pools from the mountains. Lavender, riotous red splotches and dark blue streaks of it, tinted the night. The sky, soggy with color, dropped its edges upon the dark circular mountains and sagged in the middle until even the stars blinked from the heat.

When Marston awoke it was night. All his senses seemed preternaturally receptive and attuned to the silence. The desolation was utterly complete, like the deafening roar of a million dead things. He felt a bead of perspiration gather in the roots of his hair and roll past his eye and down his cheek. Down off the ledge of rock the sky had sunk into the valley until he could feel the very squish of the universe. Before him, down and out the curving cañon, the floor of the valley was terrible and magnificent to behold. It was like the frozen surface of a huge inland sea of sterile white violet, crossed by dark evanescent streaks. There were no ripples. All was flat, boundlessly deep. There was no moon. The world, the sky was one, bathed in that ghost-like pallor which permeated even his senses.

He rose to his feet in a daze and put out a hand to the rocky wall. Then slowly he turned around. From the cave below him

95

on the opposite narrow ledge a dying fire glowed faint as a fallen star. Off to one side stood the packed burro. In the dim glow of the coals he could see the recumbent forms of Arvilla and Horne. She was lying outspread before him, leaning back upon Horne's breast. His arms were around her, toying with her body. At intervals he drew her back against him and bent his head down over her shoulder.

Very faintly, there came to Marston their muffled yet resonant tones. In all that silence the voices dripped with a disquietude that was vaguely unfamiliar, disturbing. It was Horne who appeared to be talking, for only occasionally did Arvilla twist her face to his with a bright flash of teeth which Marston caught above them. His words, in a rumbling torrent of sound, seemed at last to have broken the barrier of months of silence. As though all that solitude, so voiceless, so fleshless, a measureless interlude through which he had waited alone, was broken with the gold of a woman's voice.

And it seemed to Marston, standing, waiting in the purple haze of silence above them that he was witness to the rebirth of a man lost to all earthly desire. A curious flash of remembrance of Arvilla came and went immediately. She seemed far distant, utterly remote in Horne's arms, a stranger to all memory, and yet it was the first night she was gone from his side.

For a long time Marston stood there, a gaunt tall figure leaning against the rocks, peering with bent head across the black deep chasm at his feet.

And then, like the last twitch of a vanishing star, all life and thought seemed gone. He felt at that moment an anguish impossible of conception, the feeling of a man who knows in every fiber of his being that he has lost his soul. He knew that he was whole, of mind and body, but that something was forever gone. Yes, suddenly as though an electric switch had robbed him of life, a lamp blown out, a human dynamo without the spark of immortality. For an instant there burst upon him a flash of the feeling he had had that to set foot in the valley was to forever remove himself from all the power of God. Past his head he heard the trickle of a few sands and the infinitesimal scrape of a lizard's foot. The heavens seemed to vibrate until his whole body began to tremble. It suddenly ceased. His veins swelled; he had no knowledge of, or care for anything.

The next moment he knew he was going to kill Horne.

Arvilla rose to her feet as he approached and hastily flung over her shoulders the black shawl. Horne looked up without greeting. He had risen to his knees and his long uncut hair was rough as the jagged shadows on the walls. His arms were bent, hands close to breast. In the pallor of the night they seemed to hold a glitter, long and white, like a pale moonbeam, at which he stared mesmerically, and mumbled to himself. Yes! Here was Horne, as though inside a dream, a fantastic figure with the heart of the world for a realm. Yes, here was Horne, the man of dreams that Marston had painted with nights of a thousand thoughts. Ragged, unshaven, patches of his toil-twisted body still covered with bits of skins, he was kneeling hands at breast as though in supplication.

How did Marston himself appear; how else could he appear to this creature lost so long in the dark, impenetrable gloom of his own thought—a fantastic, unreal figure himself brought by Arvilla from over the horizon Horne's mind had long forgotten, whose hands had crystallized the dream of gold. Horne only knelt, muttering, stricken, like a pietist before a priest. And over Marston there swept a vast feeling of revulsion for the man before him.

"You wish gold now, Le' Marston?" Arvilla asked.

She lifted a small sack of crushed ore to him but Marston did not turn his head. In his manner was something ominous; he stood, calmly, with no movement save for his eyes. Arvilla looked at him queerly, and followed his gaze toward Horne.

"Do you not love me now, Señor, as does the Señor Horne?"

Her gaze wavered before Marston again lowered his eyes.

"Did I not tell you I have patched our boots, and loaded the burro with water and a bag of little gold lumps?" Arvilla was plainly frightened. She spoke rapidly. "Soon we will leave when it is too dark for the Lizard Woman to see us when we take her gold. For it is hers, no es verdad? Hers to whom God gave the land. Ah, but sometimes I am afraid. You will take care of us, Le' Marston, who knows so many things?

"Ah, sí! And we will leave quickly this land of lizards and many crawling creatures. For will not this charm protect us again? Here, Le' Marston, you will wear this on your arm who made us the gold, who will lead us away."

There it was in Arvilla's outstretched hand, flashing with his remembrances of the first night on that upstairs porch of La Casa Blanca and the night at the old fig woman's. Again the elusive feeling of the legend seemed to enclose him within that great curving talus of stone, as though in the darkness of his mind he stood in the shadow of the serpent above. Even as she spoke, Marston reached down and snapped it about his wrist.

Arvilla stepped back, a sudden fear holding immobile her dark distended face. Horne appeared to be trying to rise but something in Marston's face transfixed him to the floor. He was quiet. The muscles of his mouth were crawling as though to form words whose use he had long forgotten. His pale, protruding teeth flashed in the faint glow of the flames.

"Madre de Dios! Señores! It is no knife, look! Do not fight!" Arvilla cried, but Marston did not turn his eyes from the ill-concealed glitter in Horne's quiet hand. Stealthily he stooped and reached behind him, Horne's own face transfixed in a stare upon his. When he straightened, a jagged piece of ore was in his hand.

"Le' Marston! God's love! There is much gold for us all!"

Horne half rose. The man was an image, an immovable graven cast, without life. The moonbeam in his hand was a soft flower, a pale petal of light, dim, unrecognizable. For one instant he seemed to awake with comprehension. His face softened. Half-smiling, he rose and made one movement. Slow, and silent as a shadow, with an outstretched hand.

Marston stepped back, as though to escape a thrust, and struck—swiftly, with the piece of rock.

Arvilla screamed and flung herself too late at the figure outlined against rock and sky. Only for a moment they struggled,
entwined, upon the ledge of rock. Then they parted before her
outflung hands easily as figures from a screen, and noiselessly,
smoothly, one of them slipped into the sky. A cry, one vast, sad
reverberation of anguish and betrayal rose from the deep pur-
pureal darkness of the rocks, and all again was silence. She rose
to her knees, eyes staring to see which of the remaining figures
was rising from the ledge and turning toward her.

"Le' Marston!" her voice quavered, throbbed, infinitely deep,
as she threw herself forward. "Oh, Señor, it is you!"

Marston struck her to the ground and leaped for the burro.
Yet far up the cañon that cry remained in his ears with all the
taunting cruelty of the dread figure upon the rim of rocks above
him, all the hopeless fearful pallor of the night whose shadowy
fingers reached out to grasp the rawhide thongs of the cuarta
with which he lashed the burro,—"Señor, it is you!"

For as he struck, he had seen in Horne's outstretched hand
only the pale flash of a glass test tube in which still remained a
whitish paste of gold and mercury amalgam.

✳ VII ✳

SEATED ON THAT WHITE-WASHED, upstairs porch of La Casa Blanca,
Lee Marston's face stood out but indistinctly, yet infinitely sad,
through the dim light of the room. Across it there seemed to fall
all the shadows cast by the end of the tale whose darkness not
even the last clink of glasses at the bar, or the dying music of the
cantinas could pierce with its mixed melody of light and sound.

"Well," someone spoke from across the table as though to
show he too were awake and aware of that quiet figure, "what
was the end?"

A voice breathed deeply. In the darkness of that quiet, upstairs porch, they were but voices only, who with a spoken
thought dropped again to silence. From the moody gloom Dane's

The Lizard Woman

voice, swarthy and dark-shadowed as himself, rose to answer, caressing with the same repetitious sound of the hour's tale.

"There is no end to any tale. It, like the beginning, is forever shrouded in the mist of our understanding. For only when the first perception of reality strikes into the befuddlement of our senses like the first shaft of early morning from a dark horizon, do we clear our eyes and say of what we see, 'This is the beginning.' So for this tale, like all tales, there is no end. Like an endless wave of sand, it but rises to a crest, falls swiftly in the gathering darkness, and is lost in the unfathomable gloom of our shadowy minds."

"Oh, come, Dane. Even you don't know what he thought. Tell us what happened at the end."

"The end? Can I say, having but told you the facts? Can you? No. There is but one end. There he sits, and here has he lived, alone yet not solitary, and about him hangs the past as a low-hanging mist forever hiding the sky of his dreams. What can I know, having only found him on the very edge of things, on that indefinable border of your world of facts and the nameless, chaotic, lonely region of forgotten things which is the desert to Lee Marston?"

A glow lighted his reflective face for an instant; and then with the cigarette which seems in his hand so ridiculously small, he began again. "Yes." And then once more, "Yes, I wonder if he'll ever know. In all our talks he stops short of what you say is the end. They found him just ten miles out on the desert and the burro out six miles more with the sack of gold still tied round its neck like a bell and bloated beyond all recognition. How he ever got out I don't know. Think of it, the appalling, overwhelming actuality of it. That figure curled over the rocks, her tenuous body outlined like a sleeping purple shadow in the green phosphorescence of the night sky. Arvilla's scream! How that must have reverberated in his ears, echoing like the breathing of his own labored exertion up the steep sides of the pass. He was talking about her with those first words of his after his tongue had dried to normal size. They found her at the first range of hills—

100

you must know how, buzzards and things. All that way after him, following with that dogged determination of hers, a relentless will, and outstretched arms, as if at the last she had found one path without a turn, without a thought for gold." . . .

The door opened suddenly and in the flare of light he leaned forward and beckoned to the shuffling Chinese. "Hen'y, you'd better run down the street for another bottle of wine. No, not that stuff from the bar below us; you run along down the street. And, Hen'y, will you stop at the table inside when you come back—yes, the young man with the brown face and light hair—and tell him that I—you know me, Hen'y—that I shall wait with the wine for him. Yes, that'll do to tell him, Hen'y."

He slipped back to his chair and darkness. "What?" we heard him ask. "Oh, no. By the time he could act sane and think straight, summer had passed and Arvilla was long buried—Hang him? Why? They couldn't find where he'd been. They never found Horne; and so they call him crazy behind his back, and laugh at his 'Arvilla, the Lizard Woman.' But there you are! Plain murder if you will. Two men and one woman. Two men and gold. That's what you say. What I say is neither. What I tell you is that something, a real inexorable embodiment of that omnipotent structure of creation which existed before God created man, filled his soul with a force he was powerless to stem. Of that I am convinced."

His voice died slowly as he turned to watch Hen'y coming across the now deserted dance floor and stopping at Marston's table. He turned to us quickly.

"I hope he comes. But not for you. Remember me as you will, but of him I am sure you can take nothing but the essence of the spent spirit of your untroubled youth. I hope only for him that from you, like myself, he can get once again the sense of others, the crowded sense of hurry, the allures of the unattainable which are of your life.

"Here he comes toward us. Please remember him, please forget the damned, blind facts just this once. Be charitable if he talks, be kind."

A shadow fell across the table. A blur, a silhouette in the doorway.

"Come out where it's cool, Marston," came Dane's voice; "it's a corker of a night, and we're going to have some Spanish Moscatel and hear about the world we've forgotten, you and I."

Marston, without a word, opened the swinging screen door and ambled to our table with that effortless, slow gait of his. And in the thin cone of light filtering through the torn canvas of the door which was softly closing after Hen'y, we saw a cheap brass bracelet, such as may be bought as any souvenir, upon his bare brown arm. Yet it was beaten in the likeness of a lizard, whose tail was wrapped about his wrist, and whose head was the face of a Mexican dancing girl. And at its sight, all that silence, all the tremulous fitful noises of the street below, seemed like the peopled voice of the solitude about us, forever crying in our ears. . . .